# 25th Pan Book of Horror Stories

Herbert van Thal compiled a number of anthologies including some of the writings of James Agate, Ernest Newman and Hilaire Belloc and a volume on Victorian Travellers. He also resuscitated the works of many neglected Victorian writers. In 1971 his autobiography, *The Tops of the Mulberry Trees*, was published, as well as *The Music Lovers' Companion* (with Gervase Hughes). He also edited Thomas Adolphus Trollope's autobiography and a two-volume work on Britain's Prime Ministers. He died in 1983.

D0761296

edited by Herbert van Thal

# The 25th Pan Book of Horror Stories

**Pan Original**
Pan Books London and Sydney

This collection first published 1984 by Pan Books Ltd,
Cavaye Place, London SW10 9PG
9 8 7 6 5 4 3 2 1
© Pan Books Ltd 1984
ISBN 0 330 28206 9

Photoset by Parker Typesetting Service, Leicester
Printed and bound in Great Britain by
Hunt Barnard Printing, Aylesbury, Bucks

This book is sold subject to the conditions that it
shall not, by way of trade or otherwise, be lent, re-sold,
hired out, or otherwise circulated without the publisher's prior
consent in any form of binding or cover other than that in which
it is published and without a similar condition including this
condition being imposed on the subsequent purchaser

# Contents

# Acknowledgements

Terry Jeeves c/o Pan Books Ltd, Cavaye Place, London SW10 9PG for 'Upon reflection'.

J. I. Crown c/o Pan Books Ltd, for 'Josie comes to stay'.

Norman P. Kaufman and his agent, London Management Ltd, 235, Regent St., London W1, for 'Just one of the family'.

Curt Pater c/o Pan Books Ltd, for 'Jobcentres are less dangerous'.

Ian C. Strachan c/o Pan Books Ltd, for 'The architect's story'.

Alan W. Lear c/o Pan Books Ltd, for 'Let's do something naughty'.

Christina Kiplinger c/o Pan Books Ltd, for 'Grave business'.

Alan Ryan c/o A. P. Watt, 26/28 Bedford Row, London WC1R 4HL for 'Onawa', 'Tell mommy what happened' and 'Baby's blood'.

'The boogeyman' and 'The woman in the room' taken from *Night Shift*. © 1976, 1977 and 1978 by Stephen King. Reprinted by kind permission of New English Library Ltd.

Barbara-Jane Crossley c/o Pan Books Ltd, for 'Black silk'.

Carl Shiffman c/o Pan Books Ltd, for 'The squatters'.

# Alan Ryan
# Baby's blood

'It's called Baby's Blood,' the man said. 'Taste it.'

Mike the barkeep cocked his head to one side, drummed his thick fingertips on the bar in front of him, and looked speculatively at the stranger.

'Go on,' the man said pleasantly, an understanding smile flitting across his face. 'It won't hurt to try. Just have a sip and tell me if it isn't different from anything you've ever tasted before.'

A hard-edged shaft of brilliant sunlight stabbed through the narrow window at the front of the bar, but the interior of the place remained dark and gloomy, as if resisting the onslaught of morning light from the outside world. The heavy wooden tables and booths shone dully beneath dim light bulbs, and the long wooden bar itself glowed as if it was still damp from last night's business. By night, the place offered Mike's regulars and the sometime drinkers a haven of warmth and glowing yellow light to hold at bay the emptiness of these spring evenings; but by day, and especially by morning, the place seemed, almost felt, chill and dark. A night-time place, for sure, and the dazzling light outside succeeded only in peeking hungrily through the window.

It was for this reason that Mike the barkeep had decided seven years ago, when he first came to this country from the other side, that he would not open his place until two o'clock in the afternoon. Sure, many of his countrymen, fellow owners of taverns, opened up at eight in the morning, but that wasn't for Mike, it wasn't his way. If he couldn't keep a bar and make his fortune on it by selling beer and liquor during the hours when drinking was decent and proper, then he wouldn't do it at all, he wouldn't. He'd told that to everyone from the start, and he'd stuck to it. And to tell the truth, besides, he couldn't say that he much cared for the inside of a taven in the morning hours, his own included. A tavern was too dark, too gloomy, in the morning, with too many alcoholics coming in to drink their breakfast while the missus cried at home.

No, that wasn't the way for Mike. And he was satisfied. He lived like a decent citizen and a good family man in a nice house with a garden over in Riverdale (and wasn't it a crying shame his father, God rest his soul, hadn't lived to see *that*), his two girls were in a good Catholic high school, he seldom had to deal with drunks, and there against the mirror, right over the cash register, was the handsomely painted sign that proclaimed for all the world to see: 'Michael Walsh, County Cork, Proprietor'. Thank God for America.

But he still disliked being here in the mornings. He wouldn't have been here today, in fact, except that Tommy, his afternoon bartender, had called him at home and said that one of the kids had been taken sick and he was giving the wife a hand and he was sorry but would Mike mind going in himself to straighten up the accounts and check the stock? Well, Tommy was a good man and these things happened. But if it hadn't been for that, this stranger on the other side of the bar would be talking to Tommy instead of him.

'Come on,' the man said, 'at least you can give it a try. It certainly won't hurt to try. Just taste it and I think you'll be convinced.'

Mike let his eyes drop from the stranger's face to the small clear bottle the man had placed on the bar. It was an odd-shaped bottle, he was thinking, a shape he'd never seen before. His trained eye studied it and he guessed it held about a pint and a half. There was no label on it and that made Mike just a bit uneasy. On the other hand, it didn't put him off completely, either. He was an honorable businessman, always had been, and no one could say otherwise, but after all, a businessman had to be watching for the advantages, now, didn't he? It wouldn't be the first time Mike had tasted – or bought, for the matter of that – something offered in an unlabelled bottle with an unusual shape.

'Baby's Blood, eh?' he said. He studied the bottle. Through the clear glass, a thick but bright red liquid seemed almost to glow. Mike's eyes – eyes that could tell one brand of whiskey from another, and do the same with scotch or bourbon, in the half-light of evening in the bar – failed to get much information from the bottle of liquid. It stood just a few inches from where his large-knuckled hands rested on the gleaming wooden surface.

'That's right,' the man said. 'Baby's Blood.'

'Powerful name,' Mike said. His eyes were still playing over the bottle, his lips pursed.

'Powerful drink,' the stranger said.

After a moment's silence, Mike said, 'Don't look thick enough to be blood.' He glanced up from the bottle to the man's face, a pleasant, reliable sort of a face, he would have said.

The stranger's smile widened slightly. 'No,' he said. 'No, as a matter of fact, it doesn't, does it.' He glanced down for a second at the bottle, then looked back at Mike, and his shoulders moved in a shrug. 'Babies, you know,' he said. 'Very thin blood.'

They smiled together.

'Well, what do I do with it?' Mike asked. His fingers closed around the bottle, slid it closer to his side of the bar. It was cool to the touch and Mike thought he remembered seeing something white, maybe some kind of insulation, inside the man's sample case when he'd first opened it to take out the bottle. Mike tried again to recall where he might have seen a bottle of this size and shape before, but the memory, if indeed he had it, eluded him.

'Almost anything,' the man said. He leaned forward, his arms on the outer lip of the bar, relaxed now that Mike was actually going to taste the sample. 'Almost anything at all. You can mix it with anything. Use a customer's favourite mixer – tonic, cola drinks, lemon drinks, whatever. Or splash a little water in it. Or even a *lot* of water. Some people like to use it in mixed drinks, you know, just use a few drops in, oh, say, a Manhattan or an old-fashioned. You'll come up with all sorts of things, depending on your clientele.'

'What about straight?' Mike asked.

For the first time in their conversation, it was the stranger's turn to hesitate. 'Well,' he said slowly, 'I'll tell you the truth. We don't recommend it. This is pretty strong stuff. Now that's not to say you mightn't have somebody who'd want it straight and I'm not saying you wouldn't want to serve it that way. God knows, in this business there's no accounting for taste.' He looked Mike directly in the eye and they smiled together again. No, that was certainly the truth;

there was no accounting for taste, especially in this business. 'But really,' the man went on, 'we'd prefer to see it used with something else. That's what we recommend. Besides, there *is* the matter of price.'

'What does this stuff cost?' Mike asked.

The stranger looked relaxed again, confident just this side of smug. 'Taste it,' he said.

'And you're not going to tell me what it is?'

'Taste it,' the stranger said again.

Mike shrugged and figured what the hell, he'd gone this far, might as well give it a go. He slid the cool bottle to his side of the bar, then reached overhead to one of the glasses that hung upside down from a rack above his head. He scooped a few ice cubes into the glass from beneath the bar, then set the glass beside the bottle. With a practised hand, he unscrewed the cap from the bottle. The cap required a tight downward pressure and opened with a tiny pop. Mike realized instantly what the bottle was: one of those special jars made for home canning and preserving, with a grey rubber ring around the mouth, the kind that Paul Harvey is always advertising on the radio. Mike lifted it, held it up to the dim overhead light. It glowed red, but otherwise told him nothing. For a second, he thought he might sniff at the mouth of the bottle, but instead he just splashed some of the red liquid over the cubes in the glass. As he set the bottle down, a dime-sized drop of red landed on the bar. Automatically, Mike reached under the bar for a towel and wiped it away.

The red liquid shone bright around the ice cubes. Mike tried to judge its consistency and decided that it was somewhere midway between tomato juice and cranberry juice.

He lifted the glass to his nose, swirled the contents around a couple of times, and sniffed. Nothing. No, wait. Well, maybe just the slightest suggestion of something vaguely familiar. He sniffed again, swirled the crimson liquid over the cubes, sniffed once more. No. No, there was nothing he could recognize.

'This is alcoholic, isn't it?' he asked the stranger. 'I have no use for those damned prepared mixes, you know.'

'Just add a little water and taste it,' the stranger said.

Mike sighed. Might as well get on with it, he thought. This thing

10

will either be something or nothing, so the sooner we get on with it, the sooner I can get on with my work, one way or the other.

He reached for the head of the hose dispenser, pressed the button, and fired a sparkling stream of water into the glass. The mixture of water and red liquid foamed madly for a few seconds, then settled down, leaving a frothy ring of tiny pink bubbles coating the inside of the glass.

'Down the hatch,' the stranger said.

Mike lifted the glass to his lips. Lord ha' mercy, he thought quickly. He took a drink, filled his mouth with the liquid, sloshed it around to get the full effect of the flavour. He felt, first, the coldness of the drink, then felt it warming slowly in his mouth, but he could discern nothing by way of a distinctive flavour. He waited a few seconds longer, letting his mouth warm the drink a little more to see if that would release the taste, then sloshed it around again, searching now for the right area of his tongue that would report the taste it found. He waited, but he still wasn't certain that there was any taste at all.

'Have a little more,' the stranger said.

Mike, committed to going along with the man's request now that he had started, swallowed the mouthful he had and lifted the glass to his lips to take another. As the first mouthful slid down, he thought he detected, as if at a great distance, a familiar and comfortable warming sensation in his gullet, right down the middle of his chest, but still, he couldn't really be absolutely sure. It might just be an automatic reaction to taking a drink; the mind could play tricks on a man, after all. He filled his mouth a second time, leaving, he noticed, a streak of frothy bubbles, pale pink in colour, up the inside of the glass. As before, he tossed the drink around in his mouth and waited for some sensation to reach his brain. The stuff must have some taste, he thought, it must taste like something, unless the stranger was trying to sell him coloured water. But no, it couldn't be that, he thought at once, the stuff, whatever it was, was certainly thicker than water. He sloshed it around again in his mouth and waited.

The phrase he had just thought echoed for a moment in his mind. Thicker than water. Blood. Baby's Blood.

He swallowed abruptly, hesitated for a second, then cleared his throat and said, 'This isn't blood, is it?'

'Baby's Blood,' the stranger said, his pleasant, patient expression unchanged. 'We call it Baby's Blood. Take some more. You won't have long to wait.'

Mike sighed quietly once more. In for a penny, he thought, in for a pound. He took another mouthful from the glass.

This one seemed somehow different. Warmer. Thicker. Richer. He was just barely aware, at the outer edge of his consciousness, of a hint of something metallic. And maybe a suggestion of . . . the ocean? Salt? Yes, maybe a slightly metallic taste. And the warming effect was growing, yes, he could feel that now, not only in his mouth but in his chest and stomach, as if the accumulation of liquid he had so far swallowed was painting the inside of his body, coating it thoroughly with its red and glowing warmth. And something else. It felt good in his mouth, without actually tasting like anything in particular.

'Very interesting,' he said, after swallowing the last mouthful.

'Take one more drink,' the stranger said.

Mike lifted the glass again, noting – was that a tiny twinge of sadness? – that it was almost empty. There was just a light coating of pink, with a tiny pool of darker red at the bottom, the spot of colour magnified and distorted by the ice cubes. When he filled his mouth this time, the drink felt – tasted? – very pleasantly warm, surprisingly so, because the ice should have cooled it. And then, too, he remembered, the bottle itself had been cool when the stranger placed it on the bar. But this mouthful already seemed warm when it entered his mouth, as if it had been warm all along. Very pleasantly warm. In fact, Mike was beginning to think that he liked it a lot more this way, warm, than he had when it was cool, like that first taste he'd had. Yes, it was definitely better warm. He looked down into his glass and saw that a final drop had collected at the bottom. Oh yes, it was a very interesting drink indeed. He swallowed what was in his mouth and, lifting the glass one more time, drained off the remainder. Warm, the drink was warm now and sending warmth all through his body. The back of his neck felt warm. Mike was feeling by now very confident of his ability to recognize a good thing when he saw it or, for that matter, tasted it. Yes indeed. It was a fine drink, a very fine drink. He was quite warm now, yes, but feeling very, very good. Reluctantly, he let the last of it slip down his throat and looked with mingled regret and satisfaction into the empty glass.

'Baby's Blood, eh?' he said, letting his eyes meet those of the stranger. He cleared his throat. 'I'm just wondering,' he began, 'do you have to be calling it that? Maybe some other . . .'

'Baby's Blood,' the stranger said, his voice flat but smiling still.

'Ah,' Mike said.

A tiny silence hung between them.

'Well,' Mike said, his breath almost a sigh, 'it's different, all right, isn't it? Almost like you'd imagine.'

The stranger's nice smile never wavered. 'Almost,' he said.

'The genuine article, I suppose, of course?' Mike said, raising one eyebrow at the man across the bar. 'Or are there added ingredients?'

'Maybe just a little something added,' the stranger said easily. 'But consider it the genuine article.' His smile broadened ever so slightly and he added, 'For all practical purposes.'

They smiled, understanding each other, businessman to businessman.

'I see,' Mike said slowly. 'Well.' He ran his tongue around the inside of his mouth. The soft and quiet warmth the drink had induced flowed gently throughout his body, bringing a comfortable glow to his stomach, his groin, his legs. The sensation was like nothing he had ever felt before, warmer and somehow deeper. His fingers slid across the smooth surface of the bar and lightly touched the bottle. It still held, he estimated with a hopeful glance, enough red liquid for . . . oh, for quite a number of drinks. The tips of his fingers were tingling pleasantly now, a sensation he hadn't felt since the very earliest of his drinking days. 'I see,' he said again. Remarkable, he thought, how, despite the obviously potent effect of the drink, it did nothing to impair one's speech. His fingers caressed the cool glass of the bottle. 'And just what would you be asking for a bottle of this Baby's Blood?'

'The price is high,' said the stranger.

Mike nodded. 'I was thinking you might say that. But it's a fine drink, a fine drink indeed.' Oh, he felt good. 'How much would you be asking?'

The stranger told him.

The price he mentioned was so high that, for a second, despite the overwhelmingly comfortable effect of the drink on his mind and body, Mike wondered if he had heard the man correctly. But in the next second, he knew he had, and in the next second after that, he knew the price was a fair one. Before he even realized what he was doing, his mind was calculating the price of a bottle, the quantity of its contents, the number of drinks that could be made from a single bottle, the amount he would have to charge per drink, and who among his trusty regulars and friends would be willing and able to pay such a price. And, he added to himself, who among them would be worthy of such a drink as this. All the while he stood there thinking, leaning comfortably against the bar, the effect of the drink was spreading even more cosily through his body.

'All right, then,' he said. 'I'll be taking it.'

'Have another drink,' the stranger said, smiling even more nicely as he lifted the bottle and poured. 'This one's on me.'

The man let his car roll to a carefully timed halt, the front bumper coming to rest precisely over the painted stop line in the road, as the traffic signal above showed a combination of red and green. He could have slipped through the light, and he knew it, and he knew too that a lot of drivers would have just kept going, or even hit the accelerator to speed up and make the turn, but he was the kind of driver who always obeyed the traffic regulations to the letter of the law. Let the speed demons waiting behind him to make the turn grumble as much as they wanted. The law was the law. He glanced into the rear-view mirror and saw a kid in a green Skylark giving him the finger. The man shifted his gaze away to the traffic facing him on the other side of the divider and the traffic signal swinging overhead in a gentle spring breeze.

He sat patiently until a green arrow indicated he could make the turn, then swung the car left across the road and into the parking lot of the shopping centre. He drove carefully, keeping a wary eye out for less cautious drivers who might back quickly out of the parking space without first checking in both directions. Observing the posted speed limit of 15 mph, he rolled slowly between the rows of cars, following his familiar path along the yellow-painted arrows on the blacktop. He drove to the far end of the sprawling lot, towards the four-storey department store at the other end of the mall. A section of parking spaces here was labelled 'Employee Parking

Only'. He found a free space immediately, pulled into it, made certain his car was centred between the lines for his space, then shut off the engine and rolled up the windows. When he opened the door to get out, he took great care to make certain that the edge of his door didn't hit the side of the car beside him and chip the paint.

He locked the car, tested the handle, and walked briskly across the parking lot to the employees' entrance, straightening his tie and buttoning his brown tweed jacket as he walked.

By the time he reached the door, he had pulled from his jacket a black plastic card case with a shiny clear window displaying his store employee identification card. He had worked here for quite some while now but, as a security measure, all employees were required to show their cards every time they entered the building for work. The store had a policy of rotating the guards at the door every couple of days, in order to keep them from getting to know too many people by sight and getting too friendly with them. An extra precautionary measure and, the man thought, a good one. You couldn't be too careful these days.

At the door he flashed his card, the guard glanced briefly at it and nodded, and the man hurried inside. He paused at the time clock to punch in and quickly compared the time on the face of the machine with that of his own watch. They agreed. Good. He thought for a second. Yes, he would have just enough time to make the quick stop he had planned before reporting to his post. There were just a few things he had to pick up before starting work today.

He left the employee area and took the escalator to the second floor, standing patiently as it glided upward and stepping aside to let a young stockboy hurry past him up the steps. At the top of the escalator, he stepped off quickly and turned right, towards the toy department.

The salesgirl behind the cash register saw him coming and greeted him brightly. She was a pretty little thing with rich dark hair and bright eager eyes.

'Hi, there!' she said. 'Good morning! Got a long shopping list today?' Her smile was warm and genuine and clearly she would have liked to know the man better than she did. She was not the only one who felt that way, and she knew it, so she tried to make her smile as cheery and pretty as possible on the mornings when he dropped in at the toy department to do his shopping.

'Oh, just a few things,' he said, favouring her with his own nice smile. 'I know where they are.'

'We have some new items you might want to take,' the girl offered. 'I can show you where they are, if you'd like.'

'I just need a few replacements,' the man told her. 'You know how quickly they get worn out. I'll just be a minute.' He stepped away and disappeared down one of the aisles.

The girl hid her disappointment behind another bright smile.

She had time to ring up only one sale for a customer before the man was back, standing quietly in front of her cash register. In his arms he was clutching six bright pink and blue baby rattles and an open box of one dozen pacifiers in shiny clear bubble cards.

'You really enjoy your work,' the girl said warmly.

'Yes,' the man replied. 'I do.'

The girl hesitated, trying desperately to think of something else to say that would hold him there. She couldn't. Well, maybe tomorrow. She'd think about it tonight and come up with something for tomorrow.

'I'll write that up for you and put it through myself,' she said quickly. 'Don't worry about it. And if there's anything else I can do, just say so.'

'I will, and thanks a lot,' the man said. 'This should hold me for a bit. See you tomorrow probably.'

The girl's big dark eyes followed him as he walked away with his arms full of pacifiers and baby rattles. Maybe tomorrow she'd have a chance to talk with him, get to know him better, let him get to know her better. Her girl friend in the personnel office had secretly checked the records and told her he wasn't married.

The man walked through the main aisle on the floor, past racks and tables of children's wear, towards his own little space at the other end of the floor. Several salespeople greeted him as he passed. He returned each greeting with a pleasant smile.

When he reached his post, there were two women waiting for him already, although he wasn't actually due for another five minutes. They smiled in recognition when they saw him coming.

Cradling the rattles and the box of pacifiers in one arm, the man pulled out his key.

'Good morning, ladies,' he said as he unlocked the door. 'Just give me a minute to get these things out of my hands and I'll be right with you.' He pushed the door open, stepped inside, and flipped the lights on with his elbow.

'Oh, take your time,' one of the women said. 'We're early anyway.' She hitched the baby she was holding a little higher against her shoulder. The infant was blinking in the bright lights of the store, its chubby little face nestled warmly in the folds of a pink blanket.

'Really,' the woman said, looking at her companion, who was also holding a baby in her arms, 'he's so good with them, especially the little ones.' She patted her baby gently on the back. 'Mine is always so sleepy and quiet for hours and hours after he's taken care of her. He just has a magic touch with babies.'

The man appeared in the doorway. 'All set,' he said, smiling warmly at the women and their infants. Directly over his head, just above the doorway, a neatly lettered sign said, 'Courtesy Babysitting Service for Shoppers.'

'Here,' the man said, stretching out his arms for the first baby. 'Let me have your little angel. And don't you worry about a thing. She's in good hands with me.'


'It's called Baby's Blood,' the man said. 'Taste it.'

Nick D'Agostino rubbed one hand across the wiry stubble of beard on his chin, then leaned forward with both hands placed flat against the cool steel of his cart. Hanging from the red and green striped umbrella above his head, a sign offered passersby 'Genuine Italian Ices'. Lined up across the front of the cart were large clear plastic bottles of syrup, all ready to be poured over freshly shaved ice: yellow for lemon, green for lime, white for pineapple, purple for grape. Nick looked at the glass bottle the stranger had placed in front of him, its red liquid shining brightly.

'Go on,' the man said pleasantly. 'It won't hurt to try.'

# Terry Jeeves
# Upon reflection

Domby Grork's only warning was the muffled rustle of swiftly moving garments. It was enough. With a lithe movement, he dodged the falling sword, scrabbled a handful of dirt from the …ley floor and threw it full into the face of his unknown attacker. Momentarily blinded, the ambusher clawed at his eyes for one unguarded moment. That was all Grork needed. His own blade slid from its scabbard, flickered briefly and the assailant's weapon was twisted from its owner's grasp to go clattering away into the darkness from which the attack had come.

Spluttering angrily as he rubbed his smarting eyes, the would-be killer suddenly became aware of Grork's sword point hovering at his throat. Its gentle yet insistent urging backed him against the slime-covered wall of the alley. Grork gave the man time to feel the first faint stirrings of hope.

'Now my friend, perhaps you may care to tell me why you offer such a poor welcome to your village?' The sword tip emphasized the words.

The villain's dirt-smeared face glistened in the flickering light from a nearby oil-wood torch spluttering fitfully in its wall sconce. By the cut of the fellow's hair and clothing, Grork recognized him as a Krasnan; a breed noted for avarice and villainy. Beads of sweat streaked their way down the grimy visage.

Sucking in a deep breath, the man gasped out, 'I planned to win the lost treasure of the hill. To get it, I first must satisfy the legend. When I heard your steps in the alley it seemed that our Lady Krell had smiled upon me, but I was too hasty . . .' He broke off in terror as the blade pricked more urgently at his throat and a tiny runnel of red ran down his scrawny neck.

'Say more!' hissed Domby. 'What is this treasure and a legend which demands my life?'

18

The Krasnan's eyes roved wildly in search of aid. They found none among the flickering shadows and weird, moving mis-shapes of the night. His terrified gaze returned to Grork and kindled with a gleam of cunning. 'If I tell you all, then will you set me free?'

Domby Grork gave a cold smile. 'Ay, that I will. Free as any man may hope to be. Come now, speak.' His sword point probed deeper as he finished.

No longer trembling for his life, the Krasnan strove to ingratiate himself. 'The treasure is said to lie somewhere on Castle Hill, once home of the mad warlock, Mordred. In his time the sorcerer gained great wealth by means of his magic, by his evil, and, some do say, even by traffic with the Devil himself. He hid it well; when he died at the hands of the outraged villagers, no trace of it was ever found.' The man shuddered as the blade at his throat made itself known more intimately. In the fitful light, the blood appeared black as it coursed more strongly.

'Come now, you joke with me,' smiled Domby in a tone which held no trace of humour. 'I saw that hill as I neared the village. It bears no castle.'

'Not now,' gasped his captive. 'Mordred and his castle are long gone. The warlock dwelt in solitude for many years, using his black arts to live beyond the normal span of man. The peasants could see his castle on the hill and its reflection in the lake below. So long did both endure, that when Mordred's foul deeds finally drove the people to destroy him and his castle, the image of its towers is said to have remained hidden in the waters below. He who sees the vision of the building must suffer the vengeance of Mordred.'

'A pretty tale,' scoffed Grork. 'But where does my death come into it?'

'Legend says that Mordred's riches may only be found by one who has slain another that very night,' gasped the Krasnan. 'I thought the tale but the muttering of old women until after many nights searching the ruins I did indeed discover a hidden chamber beneath the rubble. The place was empty, but I thought perhaps if I fulfilled the legend . . .' His voice trailed away, but Grork knew that his own continued existence was due only to his having foiled the villain's ambush. A fraction slower in his reactions, and

Domby Grork would have entered the Long Sleep whilst the Krasnan ran to seek the riches of the hill.

'This hidden chamber,' said Domby. 'How might one find it? Without such knowledge, how may I believe such a tale?'

His captive babbled frantically to avoid the stinging blade. 'Only one stone still stands erect, beside it, a flat rock. Push that aside and the entrance will be revealed. Now you know all. Free me as was the promise.'

'But certainly,' chuckled Grork. 'Free as any man may hope to be, that was the bond.' He leaned heavily upon the sword hilt. The sharp blade pierced the captive's throat. The Krasnan stiffened, blood spurted fiercely and the body slumped to the ground.

'Free as all men who would shed life's cares and burdens,' mused Domby. Stooping, he wiped his blade on the man's cloak, then straightened. 'Now, since I have fulfilled the needs of the legend by having killed this night, I may well find Mordred's riches.' Leaving the corpse where it had fallen, Grork plunged into the clinging gloom which shrouded the alley.

The moon had risen by the time he reached the lakeside. By its pale gleam, Domby could see the ragged mound of stones upon the hill. Bending his steps to the rough path, Domby began to ascend.

The Krasnan had spoken true. But one stone remained erect among the moss-grown rubble. Beside it rested a wide, flat slab of basalt. Throwing his weight against it, Grork gave a mighty heave. The stone remained immobile and a second attempt met with no greater success. Cursing the dead Krasnan, he sank down on the stone to rest. Black clouds scudded across the moon, but in the moments when it shone clear Domby saw a swathe of crushed weeds beneath his feet. Understanding dawned. Moving to the other side of the stone, he heaved in the opposite direction. This time, his efforts were rewarded by movement as the slab grated to one side. A dark cavern yawned where it had rested. Thin tendrils of mist curled from the opening as if reaching for Domby. They brought with them a dank, decaying smell as of something long undead.

Pulling up a handful of weeds, the adventurer struck steel to flint. The dry stems were soon alight and by the flare of the improvised torch, he peered into the hole. A flight of rough-hewn steps vanished into the blackness. Treading carefully down them, Domby found himself in a large, dungeon-like chamber. On its floor lay a few scattered tools and a large lantern still bearing a stub of candle. Domby lit it from the embers of his torch.

The uncertain gleam cast threatening shadows on the green slimed walls. Strange figures seemed to creep upon him only to leap away again as he swung the lamp. Domby settled the lantern on a strangely carved stone. Picking up a rusted hammer from the heap of tools, he began methodically tapping his way around the mouldering walls.

It was a slow job, echoes within the noisome chamber making his task difficult. Domby persisted and eventually, his efforts brought a hollower ring from one crumbling area of wall. A few stronger blows caused a whole section of the masonry to collapse. Sweating profusely despite the clammy chill of the crypt, Domby battered away at the hole until he had enlarged it to his satisfaction. Picking up the lantern he scrambled over the rubble into another, smaller vault. Cobwebs clutched at his face as if to keep him from entering. Brushing them away caused the lantern to swing and again the leaping shadows performed their weird dance upon the walls. Steadying the light, Domby raised it on high. Before him stood a web-shrouded chest. Draped across it, a skeleton. Dust swirled high around him as he stepped forward and kicked aside the bones. The smell of decay seemed even more oppressive. Domby swung the hammer, once, twice, and yet a third time. At the final blow the shattered lock fell from the chest. It rattled among the scattered bones like some strange musical device. Stooping, Domby took firm hold of the lid of the chest. A weird, eerie squeal came from the rusted hinges as he heaved it open. From within, a foul stench swirled into the chamber. The lantern sputtered violently and went out . . . but not before Domby had caught one shattering glimpse of something scabrous and unthinkable stirring and swelling within the chest.

Grork gave one scream, turned, and half-fell, half-scrambled across the shattered masonry and up the steps into the moonlight. Gasping deep, gusty breaths of the cold night air, he turned to heave back the covering slab. Before he could do so, a hideous something appeared, making chattering sounds on the stairway. That was

21

enough! Leaving the opening wide, Grork fled across the tumbled stones. Heedless of slashing brambles and bruising falls, he leaped and fought his way like a mad thing across the ruts and boulders. Behind him followed a leathery, flapping sound accompanied by the inhuman, high-pitched cackling screech he had heard on the stairs.

Lungs bursting, Domby skirted the black depths of the lake. Tripping over a hidden rock, he crashed to the ground. Whimpering softly, he scrambled to his feet and risked a quick glance behind. The hill top loomed high in the moon's weak rays . . . and there, reflected in the still waters of the lake, he caught a brief glimpse of a lofty castle. Tall and evil it loomed, towers, turrets, battlements of ebon darkness. Then the shimmering image shattered into a thousand sparkling fragments as something hideous crawled and flapped into the water. Like a hypnotized rabbit before a snake, Domby froze in panic for one agonizing moment.

That was the last thing Domby Grork was to see. Something black, noisome and not born of this world, rose chittering madly from the pool. Dripping tentacles reached out and enfolded Domby . . .

His silent screaming continued for a long, long time . . .

# J. I. Crown

# Josie comes to stay

'I bet you got tons o' money, heh, Sollie, heh?'

'Git off, gel,' Sollie smirked, shrugging his bony, jerkin-encased shoulders to dislodge the girl's playful pluckings at his sleeve. 'All my money's down here, ain't it, Ted? Spent the lot years ago!' He winked at the yellow-faced, over-large landlord of the Spade and Bucket and was obviously enjoying the attentions of the girl, although even now he couldn't quite dispel a proprietary nagging in the depths of his very cautious gut that something was wrong here and some danger might come of it.

Josie said now, 'Will you marry me?'

He opened his thin mauve-lipped mouth in amazement and didn't close it for a full seven seconds. Then he made an ostentatious appraisal of her, casting his little grey-green eyes over her from her head to her very high heels, winking at the landlord and others between times, while his smudge of yellow-stained moustache appeared to twitch.

He saw the slim figure of a girl of eighteen or so, not overly pretty – too raw-looking for that – but not unattractive either, with a fashionable long stream of red-brown hair, which she kept throwing back with arrogant tosses of her little head. But it was her eyes he noticed, that he'd always noticed when she came in here Saturday nights, sometimes with a gang of boys, sometimes with one – tonight with none. They were vast dark saucers and now the fluorescent light of the bar pricked them with mischievous white crystals. She wore a sloppy dove-grey pullover and tight blue jeans, all so clean and crisp her complexion looked quite muddy in comparison.

'Bit o' the gipsy in you,' he announced.

'So me ma says. Grandad Smith were a traveller in his younger days, and so were she for a while.'

'Well,' the landlord chipped, 'are you goin' to take her on or not, Sollie? Go on, you may as well, she's given all the young 'uns round here the runaround for years, got through just about all of 'em now I daresay. Perhaps a bit o' maturity'd control her!' The landlord and the others round the bar laughed, till they coughed on their briars and hand-rolleds.

Sollie puffed exasperatedly on his own roll-up and picked up his half-finished bitter. 'She's not serious, Ted, that's the trouble,' he sniffed. 'Now if she were—'

'But I am, I am!'

Sollie's mouth, wet and glistening from the drink, worked several times before words came. 'All right,' he said at last. 'All right, gel, I'll give it a try if that's what yer want.'

'Okay, that's settled then,' she said smiling innocently up at him and grabbing his left arm in her small white hands and hanging on for dear life.

'Well, that's a killpig, ain't it,' Sollie blurted to the assembly.

They were married by special licence at the parish church two weeks later, when May lay around with her promises. There was no honeymoon hotel for Josie, though. Sollie said he couldn't afford that and besides he said he couldn't be away from his holding when setting time was coming up. A reception was held at the Spade. It began as a small nervous affair, with only two of Sollie's drinking pals there, her parents and her three sisters. But more of the girl's relatives kept turning up – when Sollie didn't even know they'd been invited – and in the end the Spade's saloon jumped with sweating faces and bawdy song. 'Christ, them gippoes can't half drink, can't they?' Sollie grumbled finding himself digging in his pockets for one round after another. He got out as quickly as he could dragging the girl with him.

They set off in his old blue Transit van to the little farm, the girl in the tan suit she'd been married in.

'D'yer love me, Sollie?' Josie asked, with an ironic raising of her thick black-as-slugs eyebrows. He didn't seem to hear.

'Your folks approvin',' he said after a moment. 'That surprised me all along.'

'They think you got money, Sollie,' she giggled. 'That's the only reason. D'yer love me, that's what I asked.' She eyed him a long time while they bucked along, then stuck out a short flat finger and traced a wrinkle down his cheek. 'Well?' He opened his mouth to reply but by then they were nearing the gravel roadway which ambled through the chocolate fields towards his home and she said, 'Christ, it don't half look a long way out sometimes, don't it? Nobody'd know if murder were committed down here.'

'You ain't plannin' to git rid o' me this early are yer, gel?' he wheezed through his cigarette, clapping her on the knee none too gently.

'Not just yit,' she said comfortably.

She lay beside him in his bed of tarnished brass. She wasn't a stranger to his bed and neither pretended she was. She'd been to the holding several times before. The first time he'd persuaded her to the threshold of his bedroom but no further. She took one look at the grey sheets, the yellowing of bolster and pillow, the threadbare quilt which he said his mother had made, poor old gel, afore she'd died; and she'd told him in no uncertain terms if he didn't get new linen she'd have nothing more to do with him. 'Gippoes' homes is always clean, if they're nuthin' else,' she announced curtly.

They'd been keeping company a couple of weeks then and he was getting very used to having her around. In fact he felt over the moon about it, in his more comfortable moments quite elated – although it had all been a bit difficult at first with the bachelor's life as ingrained into him as dirt in his hands.

Now he said to himself that he'd never really given up hope of marrying, though when he thought a bit deeper he realized this could have proved a bit difficult since he studiously avoided anywhere where women congregated in quantity. He knew what people said, of course – that he'd always been under his mother's thumb and hadn't the courage to get out from under. Some, he suspected, put him down as three sheets to the wind because of his innate solitariness and the fact he lived in such isolation.

The first lot were right, which was disconcerting. In the saloon bar of the Spade, not a regular meeting place of women *en masse*, he'd felt – yes he had to admit it – a certain safety. When he was going through his seemingly amused appraisal of the girl he'd been trying to overcome his terror of women, this one in particular after her terrifying question. The only excuse he could find afterwards for his awe-inspiring temerity was that he'd let a sudden, getting-rarer twinge in his loins carry him away . . . and he hoped the twinge would last.

Now he couldn't refuse her anything, and the next Saturday they went out shopping and bought a host of things. He knew too she looked askance at the peeling and soiled tobacco-brown paint of the little wooden bungalow but she made no comment on this so he maintained a prudent silence.

They lay among pristine white linen, under a quilt of powder blue, he on his side with his eyes closed, breathing steadily, she on her back, big black eyes wide, looking at nothing. Suddenly she turned to him in a swirl of bedclothes: 'I'm your wife now ain't I? – Now you gotta tell me where all that lovely money is!'

His eyes flickered open. He grunted: 'Ain't no money.'

'There must be, Sollie,' she said giggling companionably. 'A feller your age, what are yer, forty-two, three? A bachelor, livin' down here all yer life with nuthin' to spend it all on. Savin' it won't do you no good, Sollie me old friend. Might die all of a sudden and leave it all. We might as well have a good time on it now, me and you, heh?'

He swept his thick hand over his thinning, greying hair and yawned. 'Ain't no money.' He turned towards her and tried to slide his hand under her nightdress but she grasped it and threw it back at him. 'Come on, love, it is our wedding night,' and he slid it under again. 'Won't git none o' Sollie's money if Sollie don't git none o' that,' he said with a dry chuckle.

'Shy 'uns is the worst,' she said.

She stood at the stable gate, beside the highest and widest elder bush she'd ever seen, that grew up the gearhouse wall almost hiding the pink, anaemic-looking brick of the building. She plucked a disc of cream blossom from it and put it to her slightly hooked nose and drew in its sweet opiate scent. He noticed her there when he came out of the gearhouse about to give the horses their breakfast of oats and chaff. He emptied the tin scuttle into the wooden manger and waded across the deep, soiled straw-bed of the stable, smiling, the empty scuttle under his arm.

'Christ, you don't half look pretty this mornin',' he cooed. 'The low ol' sun catching your hair like that, turning the top of it like gold, that flower at your lips. You know I'm kinda fond o' yer, don't yer, in my way . . .'

'Should think so an' all! After I cleaned and washed for yer, made yer bed, proper little slave I bin. Fed you, got some real good meals, better 'n you've had for God knows how long—'

'And all in three weeks,' he said, smiling indulgently on her.

'Them,' she said nodding towards the two big, heavy boned shires munching their breakfast contentedly. 'God, you just *must* be the last in the whole wide world to use horses for farmwork. You ought to git up to date, Sollie. Git yerself a tractor. Don't need feedin', don't need muckin' out . . .'

'Hosses'll suit me. Don't pad the fields down like the tyres o' them tractors, and cheaper 'n bloody tractors too. And strong as hosses,' he added, cackling at his own joke. Then: 'Drew the tater rows out in the ten-acre yisty, putting the fosset on today. I got a load o' women comin' later in the week for a bit o' tater settin'—'

'With a machine?'

'No, ain't got no kinda machine for that. They'll do it by hand like they always done. You'll have to come—'

'I ain't then!'

'You are, my girl, and don't you forget it! You gotta work for yer Uncle Sollie if you're takin' some of his money. The honeymoon's over. You can git yer back down like the rest. You can have mother's overalls and well 'tons and that bonnet o' hers if it's hot, to keep the sun off yer tender little neck.'

She threw the flower down and stamped her foot. 'Ain't then, I tell yer!'

'You got a lot to learn,' he said.

She went but promised herself she'd not stick it for long, and each twinge of pain from her back when she straightened up did wonders to reinforce her intentions.

For a week after they were married he hadn't been on the fields at all, but had pottered about the yard not being away from her for more than a quarter of an hour at a stretch. It gave her no opportunity to search. She cleaned the house – she just had to – but in between times would sit gazing into space and wishing she could love him, just a little, but such feelings were hard to find. At odd moments she felt the greatest of traitors to him, for she'd found he had a softness deep down when he chose, a capacity for sharing that must have been as much a surprise to him as it was to her. But he wanted his pound of flesh, like the potato setting, and he was tight, and her mind locked on to this insular, flinty side of his nature and her heart cried against such treatment.

'That's the husband for you,' her mother had said, heaving up her weighty bosoms with her flat, flabby, freckled arms. 'He must have a fortune stowed away on that old farm o' his somewhere. Only ever been known to spend a bit at the pub of a Saturday night. Lived with his people all his life, no board or rent to find you can bet. They say he keeps it in old biscuit tins, them big sweet jars and the like, under his mattress as well no doubt.'

They stood at the door of their terraced house, watching the road, as her mother often did. The house was kept quite reasonably but her mother said she couldn't take much interest in a house when she'd been used to a van, although the girl couldn't remember ever living in a van, and Grandad Smith, who'd been a traveller, had died twenty-five years ago and Grandma a year afterwards. Her mother seemed to get great pride out of telling people she was once a traveller and she was full of tales of the privations of gipsies – how they'd been turned off land they'd always regarded as common ground, by greedy councils and greedier farmers; the suspicions they always came under wherever they went, whatever they did; how gipsy kids were regarded as thieving ragamuffins only fit for obscene abuse from 'normal people'. How her father – who never said much on the topic – decided to give up that way of life and get a house to gain some sort of acceptance – which, the mother said, chucking her breasts with her folded arms, had never completely happened. 'Curses on gippoes, that's what there is, if you ask me. Come from India and bin cursed ever since,' she'd conclude with great satisfaction.

The girl had listened to the tirades for many years and in her heart she began to feel pride too in her apparent heritage, and a sharp anger and brittle resentment broke out in her towards those 'normal people', farmers especially. And she had to try not only to be as good as her neighbours and contemporaries but better: thus her passion for cleanliness.

They'd just watched Sollie pass in his rusted van, his eyes glued on the road as if the vehicle was likely to bolt. Although her mother was joking, in her way, it set the girl's mind in motion. She'd longed for something different for a heck of a time. It wasn't that the local boys bored her now; it was just that they'd always been of passing fancy anyway; and the mention of money, for which her mother said she had more than an ordinary liking, brought a joyous adventuring resolution to her heart. She'd set her cap at this silly old bleeder, grab his loot at the first available opportunity and skedaddle with it (although where exactly she was going to skedaddle to had her wondering). She knew she'd have to marry him, but that obstacle had proved very easy to scramble over.

She was not, however, quite as shallow as she led herself to believe in the first instance, and even a little afterwards hoped she'd learn to like him a little, for something in her, some smooth edge to her prickly passions, wouldn't allow her to be totally ruthless. But closeness was bringing more contempt than love she found.

When she'd made the bed the morning after their wedding night she'd speedily raised the mattress but found nothing but springs underneath. She'd felt all over the mattress itself, but the feather mattress seemed full of nothing but feathers. She shone his torch beneath the bed but found only furry balls of dust, not hosts of biscuit tins, and afterwards she'd thought herself a little ridiculous. She made quick dashes into the other rooms, the so-called front-room which contained an old grey suite and a dark heavy Welsh dresser which she was quite unable to move but in which she looked, to find some bits of cutlery in the drawers and in the cupboard little but a sewing box, some balls of purple wool, some magazines on farming as old as time, and a few glasses misty with dust. She peeped under the carpet but there seemed nothing – the floors were of brick and she could see no suspiciously loose ones.

When the potato setting was over he wanted her to help him drill his wheat. But the morning they were supposed to start she complained of a bad stomach and though he gave her a glacial look he agreed she should rest a bit. That morning she allowed him a good two hours to get the horses and drill ready and get down to the fields, then she began a real search. At last!

She sought in all the cupboards in all the rooms, and there were many cupboards, mostly home-made. Then she got his torch and a stepladder from a barn and climbed into the bungalow's shallow loft but discovered nothing but a cardboard box full of Dinky toys, and cobwebs and roofbeams. She looked in the brick-built washhouse stuck to the back of the bungalow. But although the place was huge and full of junk, she found nowhere – in recesses, under piles of boxes and bags – in any cavity, any container that could have been used in anyone's wildest dreams for precious money. And the floor was solid concrete.

She discovered not a penny anywhere, even when she went through the pockets of his jackets and trousers hanging from brackets screwed to door backs. At nights when she went to bed before him – and she often did to escape him, his smell and his parochial chatter – she'd pound her little fists into her pillow in tearful frustration.

She also sauntered among the farm buildings, poking and praying, although with little hope in her head that she would find anything valuable out there, which she didn't. She often noted in the pasture back of the stables two poultry runs, made out of stackpegs with wire netting fastened round and over them, with an old home-made wooden gate at the end of each. They were empty now but it was obvious what they had been. Sollie said he used to keep ducks in one and geese in the other but there was no money to be made out of either now, from the fowl or the eggs, so he'd given the project up several years ago. Josie puzzled her mind over another use for the runs but she couldn't think of any. They already had a few pigs and a few hens for eggs for the house and she certainly didn't want any more poultry or animals to look after, which was the job he gave her after she complained often of not feeling too well.

A warm evening in late August she told him she was pregnant.

For half a lifetime, or so it seemed to her, he sat and stared blankly, uncomprehendingly at her, while she thought she could see his old brains creaking over. But then his lips stretched across his nicotine-fringed teeth in a caricature of a grin and he jumped up and took her in his arms and hugged her to him till the earthy smell of

30

him made her almost retch. He smelled her hair and swung her round the kitchen, then placed her gently on her feet, as if she were fragile as an egg. She saw tears trickling down his cheeks, leaving glistening tracks, like snailtrails, and she thought him pathetic. But she brushed his hair back once and said, 'Happy?' Nodding quickly, jerkily, like a mechanical toy, he said he couldn't begin to describe it and his face seemed to grow broader with pride.

'And it'll be a boy!' he proclaimed. 'I can feel it. He'll be a big strong lad, you wait!'

'Now,' she said laughing. 'Now I'm goin' to have a kid by you, you just *gotta* tell me where all that filthy lucre is. I reckon you got it all buried somewhere miles deep, that's what I think,' she added casually.

He twinkled at her. 'Could be,' he said. He said no more, tossing off the subject, and slipped his hand into the backpocket of his old brown corduroys and drew out a fat bunch of notes. 'I sold them pigs the other day, remember? There, git yerself somethin'. Git a present or two, buy somethin' for the baby. We'll go uptown Saturday, see what can be done. We'll have a drink or two together up there as well.' He handed her some peeled-off notes. Then, 'When's it due, gel? When's he due?'

She hated him more in those few moments than she'd detested him ever before; because of his pitiful joy; because of his condescending attitude about the money; because he'd only given her the thinnest of skins from the roll; and because she'd yet to discover more.

She wandered through the farm buildings to the farm gate, guarded by giant old elms on either side. She looked over the land around her. She could smell the soil and she hated the soil and its smell, because she'd never been able to escape from it. Her mother and she would tell people that the only work gipsies could find was landwork – pea picking, strawberry picking, potato picking, and if you went down south some hop picking, if you were lucky. Her life had been surrounded by the soil, the fields, ever since her mother had taken her when she was a baby and sat her on the headlands among the clods and ridges to play the day away. The smell, the primitive, hostile, implacable smell had entered her nostrils then and been there ever since. She detested the earth as a living, tyrannical being.

Now she seemed trapped worse than ever. She wandered back and went to the stable gate and whistled the shires over. She would often come here to console herself with them. She admired the great beasts and curried their favours. She brought them cubes of sugar and pieces of the cake she made herself – when she could persuade Sollie to take her to town to get the ingredients, and provisions in general. The giant horses took the bits from her hand with the gentleness of rabbits and then nuzzled her for more, adoring the sweetness, and she would take their colossal bony heads in her arms and kiss them.

They began to know her very well. She took them on the land a few times in carts and when she clicked her tongue they'd move power-fully forward, a few additional clicks and they'd turn right or left, a gentle but firm 'Whoa' and they'd stop dead on their tracks. In the stable or pasture a short whistle from her and they'd come running.

He took her into town encapsulated in the Transit and before the afternoon was out a shining cream and black pram was perched in the back and the rest of the floorspace was covered by boxes, bags and parcels. They went for a fish and chip tea at the town's only café and afterwards, at her eager insistence, he took her to the little cinema. He said he didn't hold with TV or the pictures but grudgingly allowed himself to accompany her. He pulled her into the Spade afterwards, glad when the whole artificial show was done.

'Why don't you have a short or two?' she enjoined him, grinning and winking at the barman. 'Big celebration, ain't it? Live a little!'

He gave a lugubrious shake of his head. 'Admit I do like a decent whisky from time to time, but the stuff gives me heartburn like hell, besides getting me kalied in no time flat. But I tell yer what – mother used to make that home-made wine stuff. We'll dip into that if you like when we git home. That gits me smashed an' all but at least I'll be on my own patch then. She made some of it a good many years ago, should be good stuff now. Remind me.'

She did and then marvelled where he got it from. He went into the front room, pulled the Welsh dresser away from the wall and then plucked at the wallpaper back of it, and a small door, papered over like the rest of the wall, came away. She squinted between wall and dresser and through the door wooden steps led downwards into what seemed a short tunnel. When he flashed his torch she saw it was a small cellar-like cavern, with brick walls and an earth floor.

'Father, the silly old bleeder, made this,' he sniffed, going down. 'Thought he was important as Hitler and had to have his own private bunker. Thought he was so bloody important to the war effort the Jerries'd make a special trip over to git him. Never believe it would yer? He put a wooden shed kind o' thing over the outlet outside, attached it to the bungalow wall, looks like a privy for a dwarf. No doubt you've seen it.'

She hadn't. He slipped down the shallow stairs like a rabbit down a warren. There was scuffling and sniffing, then he came up with a bottle of rich red liquid, almost black, labelled in elderly hand-writing 'Elderberry 65' and another of a beautiful translucent gold marked 'Elderflower 66'. 'Put hairs on your chest that will,' he muttered putting the dusty bottles on the kitchen table. 'Git it down on yer.'

'And you,' she said.

They drank the first glass to each other and the next to the baby. She refilled his and again he drank and smacked his lips. 'Told yer it were good stuff,' he grinned '– if that bloody heartburn keeps away.'

Very soon he suggested they move into the front room and relax on the easy chairs. She found some music on his elderly transistor. At eight o'clock he was beginning to speak with a slur, his eyes were becoming glaucous, and he lolled untidily across the settee. By half-past his head hung slackly over the settee back and he was snoring complacently. She'd only drunk a little, for she found she didn't like the stuff a lot and the thought that his mother had had her filthy paws in it in that filthy house put her off completely.

She went to the scullery door and looked out, across the land she hated, surveyed the buildings, breathed wearily, thought of the two disused poultry runs standing opposite to each other in the pasture. It was then inspiration came, an idea that left her frightened and hot and dry of mouth. She slid her fingers into her jeans pockets: her hands were trembling. She'd get his bloody money yet . . .

She waited a moment longer at the door, to allow herself time to become calmer. In that short time she noticed, almost sub-consciously, that the wind seemed to be rising. It slapped her face

33

when she peeked out the door and the old elms were rustling their indignation.

She returned nervously to the front room. She watched her recumbent husband and smiled a little cold, mischievous smile. She glided out after a while and went over to a barn across the yard and fetched out a wheelbarrow she'd spotted there and wheeled it to the scullery door. She went in to him again and slapped his face tentatively. His eyes opened reluctantly and didn't focus and he grunted a time or two. She said,

'We're goin' to have a little fun, you and me. We're goin' ridies. You'd like ridies, would you, heh?' He shook his head, totally uncomprehending. She pulled him to his feet and helped him to the scullery door.

'Barrer,' he said blinking in the daylight and childishly pointing with his finger.

'You just git in that,' she said. 'You git in that and I'll take you across the pasture and we'll have a look at the horses. Love yer old horses, don't yer?'

'Love th' ol' hosses,' he slurred. 'Hosses good, don't pad the fields down like—' But he got no further, his thoughts coagulating.

He collapsed heavily down on to the barrow, almost turning it over, then sat woodenly with his legs dangling over the backboard. 'Lay back,' she instructed. 'Look here, I'll git you a cushion so you'll be able to relax proper.' She darted in and grabbed a settee cushion and brought another drink out to him at the same time. She placed the cushion on the inside of the frontboard and slowly pushed him back on to it. 'Silly,' he said.

'Just you relax there,' she said. 'We're going to have a nice little game, you'll see.'

'A game, I shee, a game . . .'

She forged across the yard with her burden, opened the meadow gate and pushed the barrow inside. He was snoring again.

She ran back across the yard and dived into the washhouse and after some difficulty found what she was looking for. She trotted back and went to the runs. The wirecutters were rusty and not very sharp but the wire netting was thin and she rapidly clipped off the net roofs of both runs. Then she tackled the backs and after that opened the gates and propped them back with a couple of bricks.

The henhouses themselves had long since vanished.

She ran into the gearhouse, which was poorly lit inside by one small, glassless window, and she saw a mouse in the semi-darkness peep out of the tank where the sugar beet pulp was stored for the horses and she smiled reassuringly at it. She pulled foregears from hooks on the walls, and collars and hames, and called the big shires to her from their manger and harnessed them. She caught up several lead lines – strong cord ropes about half an inch in diameter – then led the horses into their meadow. When they all arrived Sollie was still snoring contentedly in the wind, under a sky a mosaic of speeding, bruise-coloured clouds.

With difficulty she raised his shoulders and paid one lead line under his arms, across his chest and tied it at the red flesh of the back of his neck. With some binding string she'd also brought she tied his hands together. Then she tied two more lead lines to the ends of the originals and paid them out to one horse and tied the ends to its hames. She did exactly the same when she'd tied his feet. She led one horse into one stackpeg channel and the other into the opposite one. The shires stood waiting in opposite directions, at the entrances to the runs, with Sollie in the middle, in the gap between the longitudinally opposing structures. 'You should keep goin' straight for at least a little while, heh old boy?' she questioned one horse, slapping its shoulder affectionately.

She skipped back to Sollie and looked down on him and her face was expressionless. She shook him several times and he awoke and muttered, 'A game, I remember . . .' He tried to rise but immediately fell back, felt the cords and found his hands out of operation. He was suddenly very wide awake and looking surprisingly sober, and very scared. There was a faint mischievous grin now playing on the girl's young sensuous lips.

He tried to raise himself again but she pushed him back roughly and his head snapped back over the frontboard. The left-hand horse heaved cumbersomely round, just a little, and the rope under Sollie's arms slackened then grew taut. 'Don't push yer luck,' she said. 'They might scamper before I tell 'em.'

His head and eyes swivelled round, he latched on to the ropes leading from him to the animals. His eyes opened wider than she'd ever seen them and the whites stood out phosphorescent with fear.

He tried, panic stricken, to get his hands to his left armpit to pull the rope off his head but it was impossible. The shire at his head lumbered forward slightly again and tightened it. She had put a slipknot in it and the more Sollie moved and juggled the tauter the cords grew.

'Christ, what yer done, gel!'

'The money, Sollie,' she said icily.

His eyes became understanding and sly. He sank down. 'There ain't no money. What there is is in the bank, where it should be—'

'Not with greedy old farmers like you it ain't,' she said. 'Some might be but not all by any means. You old tykes ain't so keen as that to declare it all to the taxman. Banks they can check on, cash they got no idea – right?'

'There ain't much money,' he howled. 'There ain't a fortune in farmin', I told yer afore. I put a lot o' money into buying more land, that's where no end o' cash's gone. For Christ's sake believe me!'

'You never spent nuthin', always lived here with yer folks.' She laughed suddenly, a bold, harsh sound. 'Certainly yer never spent it on clothes, nor on these bloody old buildin's – the next strong wind we get they'll collapse all of a heap, the lot of 'em. Everythin's bloody old and decrepit round here—'

'There ain't no fortune in farmin' for the little people, never has been—'

'You can do a lot better 'n that, Sollie me ol' friend! Come on, don't hang me about. You do and I tell the horses – and they're gettin' impatient, the flies is upsettin' 'em. A click o' the tongue and . . .'

'Christ no!' he blustered and she saw the tears of desperation in his eyes and he was pallid as death. 'Christ no,' he whispered harshly. He could see venom in her eyes, a yellow glow that frightened him almost as much as his predicament, and he whimpered, 'All right. All right. You got me, Jo. But after I've told yer I don't want yer to leave me. I'm fond o' havin' you around. You won't leave will you, um?'

'Tell me and I'll think about it.'

'If you go and look—'

On the instant he began talking a rotten branch from one of the tall elms at the holding gate cracked away from the trunk and came tumbling down through the tree's autumnal turning leaves. The crack was like a gunshot and lit upon the horses' ears like one, carried by the now high wind. The horses were used to most sounds of the countryside – the birds, the smack of a wind-closed gate on to its latching pillar, the roars of accelerating tractors and combines – but they'd never experienced such a sharp threatening sound so close to hand. Their ears flicked upwards on alert and their eyes rolled with startlement and fear, and the two animals bolted in opposite directions down the channels carved for them.

Sollie screamed and she turned immediately, covering her ears and face with trembling hands and hurtled out of the pasture across the yard into the house, never looking back. In the house she still kept her hands over her ears, although she wasn't sure now whether the screams continued in reality or came from inside her own head. When they didn't stop then she threw the remaining cushions of the suite together on the settee and rooted her head into them like a little pig.

Then suddenly there was no more screaming, just a veil of deep silence under the darkening buttermilk sky. But it was a long time before she was totally composed. For long enough she trembled like candleflame and her limbs wouldn't obey her. When the trauma was over she stalked about the house like an impudent baby tigress, continually throwing back her red-brown mane in agitation and frustration and claustrophobic terror, for she dare not go outside again at present.

Then of a sudden she took up his flashlight and went to the door in the front room wall, opened it by prising it with her fingers, and stepped nervously down.

She couldn't stand upright in the makeshift cellar and cobwebs wrapped themselves around her head and got into her mouth. When she swung the torch round she found the place absolutely packed with bottles, bottles stacked on the floor with bricks holding the base row; bottles on shelves; bottles in wooden and metal racks. She scurried round and found some more full of homemade wine, by their labels. She took up other bottles and these were full of glowing ruby-coloured wine – at least it looked like it through the shadowed glass – and their labels mentioned port. The labels all gave names of shippers and all gave dates. Some mentioned 'vintage port'. Many bottles of the same date were stored together and she suspected the stuff had been bought by the crate or case – and from the Spade. There were all sorts of dates; the earliest bottles she found were labelled 1955, others bore 58, 67, and some dates in the seventies. The bottles were laid on their sides and webs lay over all, like dirty skeins of thin string.

She wiped the webs away and shone the torchbeam through a number of bottles and the wine glowed golden-red back at her. But she quickly noticed the sediment that was stirred up from the base of the bottles when they were moved: great dark clots and skeins of the stuff swam round inside the dusty glass. 'Cheap bloody stuff, I might've guessed,' she muttered. She collected up other bottles but all had the scurry old sediment and some a complete, horrible crust.

In her exasperation she'd have liked to destroy the lot – fling it up into the room above for instance where the bottles were sure to smash on the hard brick floor.

But she didn't do that. Somewhere . . . sometime she'd heard something about vintage port. Wasn't vintage port valuable? Where had she heard about it? She couldn't remember, but it didn't matter. How much was it worth? She couldn't remember what she'd been told, nor when. But – she looked around her – sheer weight of numbers must make this stuff valuable. Then she knew – she'd found it. She'd found Sollie's fortune, or at least a good deal of it. There must be hundreds of bottles here – had someone mentioned £20 a bottle to her? That figure seemed to ring a bit of bell. Forgetting the lowness of the cellar she jumped with joy, exhilaration, and hit her head a resounding smack on the planks that made the ceiling. But the pain was gone in a moment. She could be rich!

And a moment later she knew her next move. She would go away, vanish. She'd load Sollie's old van up to the gunwales with the wine and she's go, go . . . she'd go to London, that's what. London was the place to get lost in, wasn't it. She'd disappear into the concrete warrens of London. She'd been there three or four times on school trips and the place had frightened her. But she was a kid no longer. It wouldn't scare her now, specially with all that money behind her. Oh no! But, really, dare she? Yes, because she must!

She tripped up the steps and out of the house, torch in hand. The old elms were not rustling but roaring now and again she received a smart slap across the face at the outside door. She had to lay on the wind to get across to the cart hovel where Sollie garaged the van. She had driven it once, although only up the roadway, but she felt confident – she'd also driven tractors and the principles seemed very similar. She had no licence but that would have to go heck.

She put the vehicle in the wrong gear for a start, into first instead of reverse, and she slammed into the back of the hovel, making the old place shudder and mortar fly from the rear bricks. Then she accelerated too fast backwards, shot out of the hovel like a 125 express. But after that she was steadier and reversed quite sedately up to the bungalow.

She began to load the bottles, first fetching separate armfuls up and laying them on the kitchen table, then relaying them to the van. But later she found a cardboard box and moved many bottles a time. She searched in the farm buildings and found a number of sacks which she put between each layer. It took her sometime and all the while the wind continued to howl. When she'd finished her clothes stuck to her and her rich hair was in black, greasy-looking rats-tails. But she surveyed the results of her labour with satisfaction.

There was only one thing she hadn't got now – hard cash. And there was only one place she knew of in these dissolute surroundings where she knew this to be. She looked towards the pasture gate and shivered and was filled with dread about what she might find.

But she must go. She'd promised herself she'd take all the money he had, and Christ! she would, she'd keep her promise if it killed her. She stalked nervously across to the pasture, finding her way with the flashlight, although the night was lit by a broad-faced moon and she hardly needed it, except the torchbeam was gold and warm, the moonlight cold and eerie.

Way in front of her, over the flat fields somewhere she heard a weak whooshing rustling sound, a sound that grew stronger by the moment. The land out there was tinder-dry, she'd noticed the other day, cracked in places and she couldn't remember when there'd been a decent downpour of rain. On the blacklands, the soil on top lay like grains of soot. The whooshing-rustling sound got stronger, came nearer.

She knew pretty well what it was. Then the moon went out and the duststorm was upon her.

She'd seen many a duststorm in the fens. They formed quickly, suddenly. They began as a small whirlwind at ground level and – people told her – the vacuum caused in the centre of the vortex by the centrifugal force of the wind sucked dust up and then there was a whirligig of dust. The whirlwind expanded and perhaps more whirlwinds joined the first and soon you had a wall of dust, brown-black and vicious, and the stuff got in your eyes, your mouth, your hair and pelted your face like a myriad of pins. The wall was totally opaque and momentarily you were blinded. You could be enveloped for a few seconds or several minutes. It was frightening. She had sat out many such storms on headlands or in potato rows. Yes, you were scared but usually the fear was short-lived for soon the storm went on its way or the wind died – but tonight's storm seemed fiercer, more vindictive and the wind higher than at most times.

She couldn't get along, the filthy stuff was everywhere; grit in her eyes smarted and she couldn't see a thing. She turned and ran at right angles to her original path and the building where the old mangel-chipping machine was housed lay in front of her.

At first she couldn't get the weary, drunken door open; the wind welded it in place. When she got it open and nipped up the stone step into the building she couldn't get it closed and lost a fingernail in her attempts. The grains of soil smacked into her face all the time and after a few moments of effort, stretching out trying to retrieve the door, she gave it up and rushed inside away from the doorway, rubbing her eyes and spitting out grit. The door slapped back and back again on to the front wall and the sound boomed across to her.

There was a strange smell about the dust, not only the alien smell of the land, but it smelt of something else, of doom she thought, and her heart turned over at the strange thought. It continued to howl in through the open door and she withdrew further and further towards the back of the building. The particles continued to bombard the place, like innumerable airgun pellets.

She retreated to the back of the building and crouched there against the rear wall, feeling in strange uncertain mood, at one moment bubbling with little-girl excitement at her audacious plan about the wine, at the next feeling panicky and apprehensive, because of her predicament, because her escape was delayed;

because of she didn't know what exactly. She still heard Sollie's screams reverberating terribly through her head and when she heard them the brain inside her little head became like a frozen block, but one through which veins of hysteria ran, likely to burst out any second. She began to shiver although she felt hot all over, specially her face after the bombardment of the dust. She ached too, as if she had an attack of flu coming on. She rubbed her agitated eyes and the lids were red and swelled, and thick, heavy tears blocked her vision; some of them, a few, for Sollie.

And her lips were cracked and felt big and Christ! she felt so thirsty. The tiny annoying particles of sand had crept down her throat and it felt raw and abrasive and curiously closed up. Her mouth felt dry as ash – dry as the dust that had permeated it, and it tasted – and again that odd term came to her – it tasted of doom, though the whole negative concept of that word was alien to her.

The dust still drifted towards her. When it had first come she'd looked for a handkerchief to block its passage to her mouth and nose but she'd found she'd only got a torn piece of Kleenex, which the vindictive wind promptly blew away. Then she had only her hand for protection and the little bits of dirt had forced themselves straightway through her fingers with little trouble. Now she looked round for a sack to use but it seemed she'd taken all of them from this building for the wine.

God, she felt thirsty. She felt she'd die if she didn't get a drink. She and her baby *must* drink . . . and all that liquid stood invitingly outside. She'd smash the tops of the bottles off if she couldn't find an opener for the corks, at least that's what she felt like doing. The stuff had all that old sediment but that made little difference at this moment. The more she thought about it the more nectar-like it became. She thought she'd give the storm about another half-minute to clear, then she'd make a dash for it.

Towards the ridge of the slightly sagging roof a moss-besmirched orange pantile rocked on a rafter. It had been loose for many years. Movement in the roof over the years had cracked a number of its mates round it and for long enough it had lain vulnerable to the weather. It had slipped from beneath its mate at the top and its contemporary to the left had cracked long ago and had moved away and the original tile's lip now clipped over fresh air. The one beneath it had cracked and half of it had blown away donkeys' years ago. There was now an elongated slit at the side of the rafter through which it would fall nicely if the wind caught it in a certain way.

She couldn't resist any longer. The dust couldn't after all kill her, could it? Then don't be so bloody daft! she berated herself. Holding her hand to her mouth and nose, her other arm straight out and pointing away from her body, with her little fist tightly balled, as women run, she scurried and crunched across the barn floor. The wind caught the underside of the tile and it began its thirty-foot plunge, lengthwise.

Primordial reaction caused her to literally rebound three inches off the floor when the tile hit her. Automatically, too, her hand came up to where the pain started a brief second afterwards, and blood and grey brain spouted between her fingers. But she never knew much about any of that.

The body hadn't finished twitching when the dust, still spuming through the door, had powdered her with streaked brown and black icing. In a few moments she was completely covered, the dust lying over her pyramidally like a newly filled grave.

Then the wind died and the land settled back under the silvery silence.

# Norman P. Kaufman

# Just one of the family

I don't know when I first noticed it: I imagine it must have been there for a long time, not as a pain exactly, nor even a dull ache, more a kind of sensation, an irritant. But nevertheless . . . *there*, lurking on the periphery of my conscious being, something alive, a tremor, a quiver, a palpitation of nerve endings, waiting to convey the message to my brain.

And then of course, once I discovered that there was indeed a spasm of discomfort, what did I do but – wait for it! – ignore it completely. Well, I mean, after all, I wasn't the type to go rushing off to the doctor at the first snuffle of an oncoming cold in the head or a tickle of the throat; I knew it and he knew it, and I could picture his scorn, albeit unvoiced, if I went to him with some jumped-up sob-story about a faint twinge that might have eventually developed into a muffled pang . . . No no, it just wasn't me; and so, like I said, I ignored it, in the hope that it would very soon go away. In fact I assumed it would go away, if only because there was no earthly reason for it to persist. For was I not the epitome of rude and youthful health? An all-round sportsman, never a day's illness in all my twenty-four years.

I ignored it, yes; and it seemed to fade. Whether or not this had anything to do with my working harder and playing harder in those ensuing weeks, well, who can tell? I would fall into bed at night and drift into an exhausted dreamless sleep, and no extraneous flutters of feeling could penetrate the torpor that encircled my mind . . . And then came the morning that I rose as usual and – the pain was there. Not sharp; not enough to make me cry out. But yet a recognizable if still-muted sting, towards the lower central region of my chest.

It would have been easy to dismiss the whole affair as a touch of indigestion, a spot of cramp, perhaps, or even a strained muscle.

But – luckily or otherwise – I had a vague knowledge of medicine, not because I had ever craved for knowledge, but simply due to my passion for active sport, and had therefore acquired a working inkling of how the body works and functions. And I knew instinctively on that cold grey morning of March last year that there was something very seriously wrong with me.

And yet – you will hardly credit it – still I hesitated about seeking medical advice. It must, in retrospect, have been some kind of mental blockage: for after all, without undue false modesty, I felt I was intelligent enough to grasp the basic facts of pathological life. But – no, I did not approach my doctor. Instead, I continued to ignore it. Or – let me be more precise – continued to pretend to ignore it.

How sensible of me, you may remark; sarcastically, of course. How profound, you may add. How far-sighted. . . Well, fair enough: I don't claim to be the world's cleverest fellow. I was merely following my instincts, which led me to recoil from illness and medication and all that goes with it. I had a horror of it: of immobility, of disease, of any type of infirmity.

In a word, if there was anything wrong, I simply did not want to know; but as the days and weeks sped by, as the insignificant ache grew into something more, as it burgeoned and blossomed into a consuming and paralysing agony, it became only too obvious that I could disregard it no longer. The pain was beginning to cripple me. I could not work; I could not enjoy sport; I could barely walk; and the anguish in my chest, constant, pitiless, interminable, made sleep all but a hopeless dream.

Murdo laid down his stethoscope and told me curtly to get dressed. I did so in silence, annoyed by the man's taciturnity, by his constitutional inability to act in any sort of a civilized manner. Christ, did he not realize that I was suffering? This was my second visit in a week: on the Thursday before, he had taken my pulse, listened to my chest, x-rayed me with a frosty and rather ancient nurse in attendance; and all the time with barely a word to me, or even to her, beyond what was absolutely necessary. I knew he wasn't just singling me out for the Murdo treatment, because this was the way he received everyone, man, woman and child, even his wife – he had a name for it, he was renowned for his manner, for the effortless way he upset his patients. But he was a good doctor. More: he was in a class of his own. And that's why I wanted him, after all: not as a life-long pal, but as a person who could mitigate this agony that rode ceaselessly along and within my body.

'Sit down,' he said suddenly. I sat, wondering what the hell he had on his mind, and not really wanting to know, because as sure as God it was going to be something nasty. 'Your x-ray pictures came back yesterday,' he went on. He gestured vaguely towards a table at the other side of the surgery. 'I'll show you them if you like; but first of all, I have a duty.' I sat there, bolt upright, my mouth drying out, my heart banging wildly as if to escape from the constrictions of my rib-cage.

'Doctor Murdo,' somebody said. 'Doctor Murdo, get to the bloody point.'

He stared at me; it was on the outermost tip of my tongue to say Sorry, Doctor; and then I thought no, why should I apologize to him, this man who's made a career out of aggravating his fellow man. I met his gaze, and his eyes were the first to drop, although I sensed that this was less due to his fear of me than to an oddly uncharacteristic softening of attitude; and the sudden transfiguration did nothing for my peace of mind.

'All right,' he rasped. 'I will, as you so succinctly put it, get to the bloody point.' He jabbed a fleshless forefinger towards my chest. 'In there,' he expanded, 'is something—' He paused. 'Something that shouldn't be.'

I blinked. 'Tell me something I didn't already know.' He wasn't even listening. He moved across the room, picked a large envelope from the table.

'Here,' he said. 'And . . . here. And here – see?' I sifted through the glossy ten-by-eight snapshots he thrust at me. They were my x-rays all right, but they conveyed little to my untutored eyes.

'You've had these specially enlarged,' I commented, just for something to say, just so that the hysteria bubbling gently just beneath the surface of my sanity shouldn't boil over. Murdo gazed at me for a long moment, his long fingers still poised over the miracle photographs of the interior of my chest. 'I see it,' I went on in some impatience. 'They're lungs, right? I know what lungs look like, Doctor—'

'Shadows,' he cut in. 'Shadows over both of them.' I swallowed; I could not speak, could not move. 'But,' he continued, 'there is something different about them, there is a curious pattern to them, one which is alien to anything my colleagues and I have ever witnessed, in a lifetime of medical practice.' He hesitated. 'Can you understand that?' he wanted to know. 'Can you not grasp the uniqueness of your – your case, young man: that it stunned and baffled some of the more experienced and competent minds in my profession?' I looked at him and then away: never had I wanted anything less than for this man to continue. 'Tell me,' Murdo pressed. 'Are you an only child?'

I looked at him as if he'd taken leave of his senses. 'I am, Doctor Murdo; and I take it the question is relevant?'

He nodded. 'More than relevant. . .' He sat back in his chair and regarded me gravely, whilst the pain in my chest seemed to shift position and grind into some fresh section of the thorax.

'The fact is,' Murdo went on, 'that in my opinion, which incidentally corresponds with that of my colleagues—'

'Yes?'

'You,' he said unsmilingly, 'have a twin.'

I sat across from him for the best part of ten thousand years and waited more or less patiently for the world to cease its frightening spin, or at least to slow down to its normal tempo. My first reaction, apart from the initial shock, was to consider whether or not Murdo was totally sane; and then, having chided myself as a fool, to wonder whether I had heard aright. And finally I had to ask myself if *I* was going mad. . .

'A – twin?'

Murdo shrugged. 'There's nothing definite. But the general consensus is yes: you have the makings of an infant attached to your lungs. One of those chance freaks of fate, you understand; a mishap when you were born, but one which cannot be laid at anyone's door. There is,' he expanded, 'only Nature to blame.' I leaned forward, only too well aware of the sweat that had formed at the back of my neck and the wells of my armpits.

'But where . . .' I swallowed hard. 'Where the hell does that leave me?'

He got to his feet abruptly; maybe my imagination was running amok, but it seemed to me as if he didn't want to face me.

'I would have thought that was fairly obvious,' he said, moving about the surgery, straightening a chair here, a book there, busying himself with a smear of non-existent dust on the desk-top. I sat there palpitating, letting my frightened eyes follow his wanderings around the room. I had to do something; I had to say something, any bloody thing—

'Maybe it is obvious,' I blurted. 'But I think I'd like you to tell me anyway, Doctor. Or is it,' with ferocious sarcasm, 'beyond the powers of my MD?' I suppose my attitude was born of a fear, a dread, such as I had never personally experienced before; but he didn't seem to mind my outspokenness. Perhaps he preferred it to an outbreak of sheer craven panic.

'Don't get me wrong,' he volunteered, his voice – amazingly – adopting an almost conversational flavour. 'I sympathize with you. I know how you must feel . . . No, please: hear me out,' as I shifted restlessly. 'Let's get one thing clear, something you'll probably think is quite obvious; but I have to mention it anyway, because you'd be surprised the number of people who either cannot or will not grasp the most apparent circumstances.' He paused, eyed me almost narrowly, as if assessing my mood, my receptivity to what was surely going to be some kind of a bombshell. 'Like they say in the US of A,' he summed up, 'I'll lay it on the line: you're going to need an operation. If you want to live.'

I looked at him, then away. An operation . . . I suppose I should have known, should have realized. Perhaps I already had, but refused to face facts. Well, I was facing them now. 'An . . . operation.' I said it out loud; it didn't seem too terrible, condensing the whole nightmare prospect into a single word: not until I began to consider the ramifications, the cutting, the scything into my flesh, the blood, God the blood— And then what? What was there, inside me? Christ—!

'Listen,' I said. 'Listen, what if I didn't need this operation, what if there's some other way, some other bloody way . . .?' He was already shaking his head; and I hadn't really expected anything else.

What was I looking for, his expression seemed to say: some tablets, some miracle medicine, some kind of divine intervention?

'Friend,' he replied. 'You need this operation.' It was an odd quirk of his, now that I look back on it: never calling anyone by their name unless it was virtually squeezed out of him. 'You need it urgently,' Murdo went on. 'Because this thing, this growth, this – this infant is growing inside you. Growing, moreover, at the pace of a normal child in its first twelve months. Which,' he added, 'is pretty damn fast.' He came back to his chair and sat down opposite me; I had the impression he was pleased to sit, and even more pleased that he'd got the worst of the conversation over with, the bit where he had to break this jolly bloody news to me. 'Not to mince words, laddie,' the doctor continued, 'I need an answer right away; so that I can start making arrangements for surgery.'

'I gazed at him. 'An answer? You mean I've got a choice?'

'Everyone,' he asserted, 'has a free choice. To live or to die.'

'Except that there's no guarantee,' I suggested, 'that I'll live if you do operate.'

Murdo inclined his head. 'Granted. But I can guarantee that if you *don't* undergo surgery—' He let the sentence hang, but made a gesture with his hands that left me in no doubt. 'You're –' he consulted some papers on his desk ' – you're not yet twenty-five. Not much of an innings if you just – well – let it all go.'

'No,' I agreed. 'No. Not at all a good innings.' Suddenly my next birthday, still a few months away, seemed a very doubtful proposition; and yet here was the estimable Doctor Murdo, expecting and almost demanding a decision from me, one that might make the difference between celebrating my quarter-century on this earth and—

I shivered involuntarily. I was not a nervous man in normal circumstances; but this. . . Here I was, a young healthy man, being asked by the doctor to deliver myself into the hands of surgeons who might or might not effect a permanent parting from my unborn twin, and who might or might not ensure that I came back to the surface again to talk about it afterwards. Christ what a predicament! I glanced across at the doctor, but he was merely slumped into his chair, his eyes still on mine, and he was waiting, waiting; he knew what I was thinking and he knew I'd have to decide one way or the

48

other, and he was prepared to sit there, the bastard, like he had all the time in the world. Which of course he did have; unlike his patient.

But there was something growing in my mind: an idea, preposterous, yes, even utterly ridiculous, but still, a notion that had come to me while I sat there thinking and sweating. For it occurred to me right then that there was a third alternative, there *was*; and if it was a concept that arose out of what might well be a temporary madness, then so be it, because it was *my* body, it was *my* life, it was *my* twin that was slowly choking me to death . . . And whilst I was not fool enough to believe that the specialists who dealt with my anaesthetized body would be anything less than sincere, dedicated people with a profound sense of responsibility for the lives they held in their gloved hands, nor was I inclined to place my own safety into the care of total strangers. It was not, I rationalized, a case of distrust; but I knew I would feel more at ease if I allowed my basic interest in bodily functions to work for me.

'Doctor Murdo . . .' He arched his eyebrows slightly, this small, dark, fiftyish man whose expertise and professionalism could not be denied. 'Doctor Murdo, I've made my decision.' He nodded slowly, but still did not speak; and there was a faint puzzlement in his eyes, as if he could already guess that something untoward was in the wind, and that my decision was far from straightforward. 'I want . . .' I paused: how the hell did I put such a lunatic fantasy into cold clinical phraseology? 'I want to live,' I told him. 'I want the operation.' His face cleared slightly, hesitantly: he knew there was something still to be said, knew that I was struggling to say it.

'But . . .?' he ventured softly. I slid a dry tongue over drier lips.

'But,' I told him, with the blood pounding in my temples and the pain tearing at my chest, 'I want to perform the operation myself.'

I suppose I could spend a colossal amount of time and use a prodigious number of words in describing the good doctor's reaction to my proposal. But I feel that such an account is rendered unnecessary: those with any basic intelligence will be able to perceive what an uproar my words caused, not just there and then in Murdo's surgery, but amongst his fellow medics later on, and in the local press – eventually the national press – later still. Words and phrases spring to mind even now, predominantly those which cast some doubt on my sanity, and in fact I was hardly of a mind to argue. How could I? The whole matter was farcical, of course it was; indeed that was the most popular word amongst the various newspapers. Farcical: to expect an untrained man to operate on himself! And there was another word: would you believe . . . madness? Madness even to conceive the idea in the first place, and to have the blind belief that it could be successfully carried out in the second place!

But I was adamant. Maybe I was mad, I told the media firmly; but at least I knew I was mad! And nothing, I stressed, nothing and nobody would dissuade me, divert me from what I began to see as my destiny. Not normally a fatalist, it suddenly seemed to me that this was something I felt I had to do, my life was in my own hands, my salvation would be of my own doing. There was no family for me to worry about, or to worry about me. I was of sound mind if not of body; I had a lot going for me in the way of intelligence and fundamental knowledge; I knew I had it within my power to rid myself of this clinging growth that was slowly and insidiously sapping the life out of me.

And if I failed?

If I failed, I would be dead. There was no second chance; and some folk would have it that there was no first chance either. But the possibility had to be considered: it was more than conceivable that I would not survive, and like every other being in good physical and mental condition, I wanted very much to live. And in those final frightful few days as I busied myself with the preparations for this mammoth, monstrous task, this self-imposed imbecility, I had ample opportunity to debate the pros and cons with myself, to waver irresolutely back and forth, asking myself the same question over and over and over and over: would I be better off under official supervision, *would* I? Or did the benefits of peace of mind, the knowledge that I and I alone controlled whatever future I had left, outweigh the realization that my lack of surgical know-how was nothing short of downright bloody criminal?

I spent those last few days setting things up, reading the books that mattered and – astonishingly enough to those who know me even slightly – praying; and then finally I was ready, with the foul excrescence within me bringing me to a last excruciating crescendo of torment.

My single room at the top of three flights of stairs had been thickly white-washed; each item of furniture, each square inch of floor, wall and ceiling had been coated with the strongest possible disinfectant. Around by bed, now divested of all blankets and sheets, I had set up a battery of mirrors, most of them slotted into metal stands, so that when lying flat on my back I would have a clear view of each and every part of my frontal body. By the side of the bed I had positioned a small occasional table, on which stood one or two necessities: such as the pressurized can containing adrenalin, for use if I went into shock; and the sterile gloves and surgical mask; and the barbiturates I knew I had to swallow, as a valuable supplement to the anaesthetic which I must inject into myself.

On this, then, the last day of May, in the first light of the early dawn, I spread a sterilized coverlet across my denuded bed, and clambered slowly on top of it . . . I wish I could begin to describe my feelings right then, whirling round my half-demented mind in a frenzy of sudden self-doubt, mingling oddly and sickeningly with the physical suffering that even now threatened to prostrate me. If there was one harsh fact that was brought home to me at that moment, it was simply this, that there was no more time to lose, not even another hour; because whatever it was inside of me, it was all but immobilizing me, the pain stopping short just this side of total paralysis, moving again like something of flesh and blood, each motion a firebrand against the walls of my chest.

Outside in the street, reporters stalked the pavement, photo-graphers prowled along with them, their faces taut and intent: I had watched them from between almost-closed curtains for many nights now, I knew they were waiting for me to call on them, so they could take my story, record this feat of daring . . . They could wait forever as far as I was concerned. If I was about to die, then it would be on my own terms: which meant alone. And if I survived, then I wanted no instant world fame. The only reward I needed was life itself.

I lay back at full length on the coverlet, momentarily riding the pain, my eyes tightly closed as I prepared myself for what I knew would be an ordeal to surpass anything in fiction. Not for the first time, I asked myself what the hell I thought I was doing. 'You mad sod,' I said out loud; and the words sounded unreal, almost meaningless, because they couldn't possibly have applied to me, now could they: because – look at me – I'm about to carry out a major operation on my own body, backed by the experience gleaned over the past few days of reading up on surgical techniques! 'You mad sod,' I said again; and reached for the anaesthetic tablets.

Then I remembered: first of all the surgical mask. And before that, the sterlized gloves.

The single naked overhead bulb gleamed yellowly along the edge of the scalpel; I stared at it fuzzily, my mind dulled by the onset of the narcotic. Had I done this right, had it been wise to take the pills prior to surgery? Or should I have relied entirely on the anaesthetic injection alone?

'Too late now,' I drawled. 'Too bloody well late now, old fruitgum.' Suddenly it didn't seem to matter. Suddenly nothing at all seemed to matter. I had taken the tablets; I had plunged the hypodermic needle into my chest, sensing rather that actually feeling the analgesic coursing through my veins, freezing my nerve endings, rendering the area of my chest cold and numb . . . I lifted the scalpel: it glittered and flashed at me, I could almost taste its lethal sharpness. 'First incision coming up,' I remarked to the empty room. My tongue felt thick, my mouth seemed to be crammed with cotton-wool; but yet, amazingly, my mind, my brain, were proverbially crystal-clear. Don't get me wrong: I knew what I was doing; or rather, what I proposed to do.

'Now,' I whispered. 'Now. Do it. Do it. Cut. Cut, you creep. Now. Now. *Now*. . .' I mouthed the words at myself in a kind of anguish; my hand would not move, and I didn't know why; I wasn't scared, I bloody well wasn't, and yet my fingers wouldn't respond to this urgent message my brain kept flashing to them. And – would you believe it? – I began to cry. Me though! I struggled to throttle back the tears, but they took no notice, they flowed and flowed, coursing down my cheeks as I realized that somehow, and despite a complete want of fear, some innate repulsion against the barbarity of this mad act was preventing me from carrying it out. It was nothing short of amazing: I *wanted* to do it, to cut myself wide open to perform whatever was necessary to rid me of the constant grinding maddening pain. . . And yet – Christ! – my hands and fingers would not function; my own inborn sense of morality, instilled in me from childhood like most other kids, the code of ethics that prevents us from defiling ourselves and our fellow man, was now – of all times! – staying my hand. It was plain mental paralysis; and I cursed at myself, and I raged, and I swore, and I cried, and I cried some more.

Picture me lying there: a grown man, sobbing his stupid heart out, one hand poised over his naked chest, a lethal blade clutched in the nerveless fingers – how can I express the frustration and the overall feeling of total hopelessness? Outside the world was going about its daily business: people with no problems beyond where to park the car or whether the boss would shout at them or if they could afford a second telly. . . But me? I had this nagging biting agony, and I felt I could have done something about it if this lunatic mental blockage had not suddenly decided to manifest itself at the eleventh hour.

I don't know how long I sprawled there: it must have been several minutes, in retrospect. It felt like hours, if not days. I seethed with the irony of it; I cringed from the reality of it. To think that my basic upbringing would be responsible for allowing my life to ebb away on a sea of unbearable pain. . .

'No!' I screamed suddenly. 'Nooooo! No No No No—!' I think I was screaming out at what fate had apparently ordained for me, and – I know how utterly daft this sounds, believe me – I tried to wave my destiny away, the scalpel scything through the air in a wide arc that ended in my face. Whether or not the anaesthetic was supposed to have spread to my head and face remained academic, because the cut did hurt me, it felt like my head was being torn from my shoulders, and I screamed out again, and again, the blood flowing copiously, endlessly, down the side of my jaw. And then, as my mind relinquished its grip on me in the face of this sudden, unlooked-for torment, my hand dropped instinctively downwards, the wafer thinness of the knife lancing through flesh and skin and tissue, biting deeply into the area of my chest.

That had been the first incision: not as accurate as I might originally have hoped, for it was little more than an involuntary slash of the blade in response to the stimulus of the cut along my jawbone. I gazed muzzily at my reflection, at the blood that surged down my chin, at the blood that welled up from the initial cut in my upper body. For some reason – for no bloody reason – I was smiling.

'Again,' I said out loud. 'Again, again . . .' And I began to cut at the flesh of my chest, not hacking at it, you understand, but making incisions in line with my pre-arranged plan, knifing into myself with all the care and attention that befits any surgeon, amateur or not. Excitement ran rampant through me: there was no pain from these lesions – my body was deeply drugged – and even the agony inside my chest, the very *raison d'être* of all these mad manoeuvres of mine, had somehow subsided a little. And I knew why, I knew it had to be anticipation that was dulling my pain: the foreknowledge that whatever came about, whatever the ending to this horrific handi-work of mine, I would very soon witness what was causing it all in the first place.

And – I would get rid of it myself. Twin or no twin.

The scalpel seemed to become a live thing in my hands, an extension, somehow, of my own fingers. As one arm would grow tired, I would transfer the blade to the other hand, so that very soon my forearms were nothing less that twin streams of gore, and my hands were slippery with my own blood, as I sliced and hacked and tore at the layers of flesh that stood between bones and the outside air. But it was *controlled* cutting; there was nothing indiscriminate about my movements, there was too much at stake for that. I had my plan – I had studied the right books, albeit for a very short time – I knew full well what I was doing, the risks I was taking.

And after what seemed like a very long time indeed, I had laid my chest cavity bare; and I gazed up into the raft of mirrors, at the reflection of the deed I had wrought, at the sponge-like organs that were my own lungs.

I stared in fascination; the texts from my books drifted across the panorama of my memory, but in this moment of truth the words seemed empty and pretentious. . . 'The lungs lie freely inside the chest wall, enclosed in the visceral pleura, and are attached by their roots only, connected in this way to the mediastinium. The apex of each organ rises up into the base of the neck, and the base of the lungs rests on the upper reaches of the diaphragm. . .' I peered intently into the recesses of my thorax, and marvelled. '. . . Th partition caused by the bulge of the diaphragm separates it from the right lobe of the liver on the right, and the left lobe, the stomach and the spleen, on the left. The outer surfaces are in contact with the deeper areas of the chest wall and are therefore marked by the overlying ribs . . .' Yes! Yes! I could see it all! '. . . Due to the main bulk of the heart on the left-hand side, there is a well-defined cardiac notch set into the anterior border of the left lung . . .'

I craned forward: there indeed was my heart, pulsing wetly in concert with the vibrant palpitation at the base of my neck. I lifted my head clear of the sweat-soaked pillow, closed my eyes for three long deliberate seconds, then opened them and looked again.

Christ!

It was there all right. This was why I had opened up the yawning cavern in my chest; this was what had so overawed Murdo and his colleagues; this was the root cause of all the pain I had endured for so long, for so very long . . .

My twin.

My twin.

I simply couldn't get it down: it was beyond belief, beyond the credence of a man such as me, an everyday kind of bloke who'd grown up in a world where certain items have no place, except perhaps between the pages of a science fiction novel. But this? Dear God Almighty, *this*?

It hung obscenely from the bronchioles that branched off from the right and left lungs, its minuscule limbs trapped amidst the clusters of tiny air sacs. It was a tiny thing, but no less vile to look upon; for Murdo had been right all along. This being was in the form of a human – with perfectly formed and microscopic arms and legs, hands and feet, now caught fast in the intricacies of my own lungs, yet feeding from my blood, breathing in the same oxygen through the walls of these sacs, where the interchange took place between the gases dissolved in my blood and the gases within the air I inhaled.

In a word, it was living off me; it was a parasite, and growing daily, almost hourly. And with its physical development would come a proportional increase in my own suffering; and soon the agony would be too much, and there was no drug in this world or the next that could alleviate it. I knew this instinctively, as I knew that this infant, this gross filth that festered within me, must be cut away and destroyed.

Yet still I did not move, could not move; my gaze drifted towards the grotesque skull, and my heart seemed to freeze over, the bile of nausea rising thickly into my throat.

It was difficult to imagine that this was the face of an infant: that for more than twenty years the foul disfiguration had laid dormant, drawing its breath from mine, an infinitesimal sphere with Lilliputian limbs, but potentially lethal, this malignant leech-child, so anxious to suck the very life out of me; and perhaps – was it so laughable? – to take me over, to build up eventually to adult proportions whilst I succumbed to the incessant nagging anguish that threatened to tear me apart anyway . . .

I gazed for long moments on the outlandish countenance, held in a kind of sickly thrall: it was a human face all right, and yet there was this nightmare quality about it, its skin drawn drum-tight across the bone structure, its ears and nose and lips so finely drawn, so perfect in detail. But it was the eyes that mesmerized me: not those of a baby, not those of an innocent being on the brink of birth, no, these were adult eyes, they looked directly at me, the faded blue irises tinged with red, the malevolence in them so manifest. God, to think that this monstrous mass was kin of mine!

And as it maintained its unwavering stare, it came to me in a sudden numbing shock that it knew. It *knew*. Its suckling exterior concealed a mature scheming mind, and it was totally aware that it was growing inside me, and that if all went well, it would usurp my place on earth, would oust me from my very existence, in the hope that somehow, somehow, it would be spared to continue its own. Perhaps preserved in some laboratory, clinically maintained and nurtured until it achieved optimum size and strength . . . All this I saw, glimmering in the mirrors above my chest; and the panic gnawed and nibbled at the borders of my consciousness, and the pain inside me, the living pain, grew and grew and filled my thoughts and drained my vitality.

But now, as if in some weird waking dream, I reached out and scrabbled for the other scalpel, the one I knew to be a little keener, a little more efficient; but my hands were still wet with the remnants of my own flesh, and with the blood and water I had set flowing from the wounds in my chest. The scalpel slid out of my grasping fingers, sliced into the ball of my thumb and toppled on to the floor in a muted clangour that echoed back my frustration. I lay there dumbly; there was no way I could raise my body from that table, not like this, shot full of drugs as I was; I would have to use the blade still clutched in my right hand, and I would have to do it now, *now*, while the last vestiges of courage remained in my veins.

In a frenzy of disgust and revulsion, I began to carve across the limbs of my putative twin, rending and ripping at the miniature sinews and tendons, hewing at the flesh and bone of arm or leg until it split asunder in a fine spray of gore. On and on I went, by now perhaps a little mad, revelling in the united power of wrist and knife as I painstakingly dismembered the loathsome object inside of me.

I left the face and head until the very end; not because of any physical tiredness, although admittedly that was becoming an important factor. No, it was simply that I wanted the satisfaction of watching that face, that hostile pitiless face, disintegrate under the wounds I would inflict on it. . .

I wish I could put it into words: the immense, almost sexual pleasure of chopping deeply into those hateful features, carving great chunks of fleshy matter from its cranium, watching as the blood billowed up from the multitudinous lacerations, veiling the deathless animosity in the watery-blue eyes.

The eyes . . . Still staring at me through the carnage, still with that look of worldly wisdom, that sage knowledge of how I felt; and maybe – was it my imagination? – with the semblance of a smile on its shredded lips . . . Coldly and dispassionately, almost disinterestedly, I stabbed into the insolent protruding ghoulish eyes, mangling them in a frantic whirling festival of steel, watching them dissipate into blobs of skin and shards of flesh and translucent jellies of vitreous humour.

It was over.

The thing was dead. My twin – brother, sister, which? – was

gone. And the pain, too, once so deep-seated, so . . . permanent: that too had gone. I had a future again.

And I had a past, too: I had the memories of something evil that had lived and thrived inside me; and of those long frightening minutes of destruction that would burn into my mind for evermore.

# Curt Pater
# Job centres are less dangerous

Mr Robbins, when he came to the door, was something of a disappointment. He didn't look in the least like someone with the power to do impossible things. His eyes were as blue and amiable as a baby's; they gazed mildly from a round pink face at the four youths.

Eddie, who was the one who had rung the doorbell, could hear Bob's feet shuffling on the gravel. He said desperately: 'We – that is, I – phoned you this afternoon.' We've really been fooled, he thought, by that guy in the pub.

But Mr Robbins was nodding and smiling, and standing aside to allow them to enter. They were ushered into a big, airy room and their host placed seats around the fireplace. Eddie perched on the edge of his chair and watched Mr Robbins settling himself in the one opposite.

'And how can I be of help to you?'

Eddie looked at his companions. Bob was sitting blank-faced. Dave was studying the fire as though he had paid to see it. Peter's thin dark face held a doubtful frown. He alone met Eddie's glance.

Eddie said: 'We met this geezer the other day. He said how you'd helped him, you know? We were hoping you might sort of do the same for us?'

The room was filled with silence. Eddie felt his face growing red. You simply did not find someone who practised Black Magic or whatever in a house like this, in a suburb like this. They must have been crazy to even expect it. Mr Robbins, he realized, was saying something.

'Oh, yes, I can help you. All you have to do is tell me what it is you desire.'

The self-assurance in his voice took Eddie's breath away. He looked again at the others, perhaps to confirm that he had heard correctly. Bob was staring at the speaker, his mouth half-open. Dave continued to look at the fire in the grate, but his eyes had narrowed to slits. The frown had left Peter's face: he flicked a glance at Eddie.

To Eddie's surprise, it was Bob who answered. 'Can you fix it so we all get work?'

Mr Robbins began to laugh, saw the expression on their faces, and sobered instantly. 'I am sorry, gentlemen. I should not have been amused. It was, you see, the unexpected nature of your request that caught me unawares. I am more usually asked for assistance in ridding a husband of an unwanted wife – or the reverse, or arranging success in business, or effecting a marriage in the face of parental opposition. Those are the more usual things I am asked for. Employment? Yes, that should present no difficulty, though I would have thought that a visit to one of these Job centre places might have been as effective.'

Dave leaned forward in his chair, scowling. 'You trying to be funny? You know how long I been looking? Three years, that's how long – since I left school. Don't tell *me* about Job centres, mister. You know what they offered me last month? A course in hair-dressing!'

Mr Robbins shook his head. 'Three years? I had no idea things were as bad as that.'

'It's the boredom that gets you down,' said Peter. 'There's just nothing to get up for in the morning, you know what I mean?'

Bob added gloomily: 'And you never have any money to buy things. Well, not enough.'

'Ah, yes. Money. You do realize that my services are not cheap?' Mr Robbins' manner had changed slightly: his features had tightened.

Bob nodded and carefully extracted a thick sheaf of notes from a hip pocket. 'Uh – how much you want?'

Mr Robbins relazed. Smiling, he named a figure. Bob looked first startled, then puzzled; he glanced at the money in his hand, then gave it quickly to Mr Robbins.

'Very well, gentlemen.' Mr Robbins rose to his feet, placing the fee casually on the arm of his chair. 'If you will come with me . . .'

He led them through the thick-carpeted hall and by way of a short

60

passage to the door of a small room. Eddie guessed that they were at the rear of the house, but the only window was completely covered with a sheet of some thick black stuff. A single bare light bulb provided the only illumination.

There was a small round table in the centre of the room, and Mr Robbins arranged four chairs around it. When they were seated he closed the door and stood looking thoughtfully at a shelf full of books. He selected one at last and turned the pages.

'Hmm . . . this one might do. He certainly proved to be powerful enough on the last occasion . . . too powerful, if anything.'

Eddie, watching, thought, It's a con. All that money we gave him like idiots. It'll take me *ages* to pay it back.

Peter had obtained his quarter of the magician's fee by prising open a car window and removing from the back seat an expensive camera. Bob had grabbed the handbag of a woman as she came out of a bank's doorway, and had been pleasantly surprised at the large amount of money it contained. Dave had sold a motorcycle which, ten days earlier, had cost him only the effort needed to start it and ride it away.

Only Eddie, more honest – or less imaginative – had raised his share by non-criminal means. He had simply borrowed it from his father. But Eddie, unlike the other three, now sat and considered the prospect of having forfeited the meagre amount of spending money left to him after he had paid his mother his board and lodging. We've been taken in by the old faker. How can he get us a job?

Mr Robbins snapped up the light switch, and they heard his voice addressing them from somewhere in the total darkness. It was an almost absurdly solemn voice, and Eddie had to stifle a sudden urge to giggle.

'Listen very carefully. If this venture is to succeed, I must have your full cooperation. First, you will take the hand on either side of you.'

Eddie reached out and felt his right hand caught and held by Dave. He moved his left about in the dark. Who was it on his left? Peter? No, he had been opposite. Bob, then. Eddie's imagination confronted him with the possibility that another hand than Bob's might grasp his: a hand with talons, perhaps. But it was a human

61

hand that took his own. Eddie let out his breath slowly.

'Now,' continued the voice in the dark, 'I want you to think very hard about the thing you desire. Concentrate on it; keep it in your mind to the exclusion of all else.' It was difficult to tell where the voice came from: Eddie thought it sounded as though it was near the floor, though that seemed ridiculous. And what was that scraping, scratching sound? It was exactly like the noise of chalk on a blackboard, and that too seemed ridiculous.

'On no account leave your places. Continue to hold hands, and remember to keep in the front of your mind the thing you seek.'

Mr Robbins began to speak strange words in a queer high-pitched tone. Eddie, trying desperately to think of what he would most like to do for a living, had lost any desire to giggle. He heard a deep clanging boom that seemed at once very far off and near at hand. It was as if a huge iron door had crashed open. Thunder, perhaps, Eddie thought: it had been a warm evening outside.

I would like to be a writer, a novelist, he thought, though these stories I wrote last year weren't very good. No, better to think of something with a proper wage – not a wage, something more like a job where people come to . . . consult. A doctor, then? No, that's not it.

Something scraped nearby. Was it Mr Robbins? Eddie felt a cold puff of air on the back of his neck, and wondered if the window behind him might be open. Mr Robbins was still chanting incomprehensibly, almost gabbling the words: there was a kind of fearful entreaty in his voice. The distant booming crash sounded again, and Mr Robbins stopped speaking at once and switched on the light. The four boys sat blinking at one another.

'Excellent!' said Mr Robbins. Eddie saw that there were little beads of perspiration on his forehead; he was rubbing a handkerchief between his palms.

As they rose from the table and trooped out after him, Eddie, glancing down, saw that a five-pointed star had been chalked on the floor. The others were moving into the hall, and he hurried to follow them. Even with the light on and the door open, this was not a room in which he cared to stay alone.

Peter had reached the front door and was talking to Mr Robbins. 'It really will work? We will all find jobs, I mean?'

62

'You need have no fear on that, my boy.' Mr Robbins' voice was richly genial. 'Whatever you had in your mind in there, that will be brought about. It will not occur at once, of course, and it may seem to take place in a natural way. But rest assured – it will be because of what took place tonight.'

Eddie saw Bob whisper something to Dave, who nodded and went out on to the path. He called back to Mr Robbins: 'Sir, I think someone has just gone round the side of the house.'

Mr Robbins hurried out to join him, an expression of extreme agitation on his round face.

'Where? Which way did he go? What sort of – what did he look like?'

'Sorry, sir.' Eddie had never heard Dave call anyone 'sir' before. 'My mistake. Must have been a shadow of a bush or something.'

Bob had slipped into the front room while this exchange was taking place; he reappeared quickly and hurried Eddie and Peter outside, calling goodbye to Mr Robbins in what seemed to Eddie an unnecessarily hearty manner. That gentleman, however, was occupied in examining the path at the side of the house.

When he had satisfied himself that there was no one about he returned to the front door. An observer, if there had been one, might have detected a certain anxiety on his face.

'He cannot have come back already,' he muttered. 'No – I know I returned him correctly.'

He hurried inside and closed the door. A few seconds later, there was a loud cry of fury from the front room.

His four young visitors were riding home on the top deck of a bus. 'It was creepy in that room, wasn't it?' said Peter. 'I mean, nothing happened really, but it was creepy, you know?'

Eddie was relieved to find that he had not been the only one to feel nervous. His disquiet had now vanished, and instead of admitting to it he said gloomily: 'Waste of money, if you ask me. The old swine ripped us off good and proper. All that money he took off us.'

Bob grinned. 'Did he, though?' He drew out the bundle of notes he had handed over to Mr Robbins.

'You pinched it back?' said Peter admiringly.

'Course I did. What d'you think all that caper was for, with Dave keeping him talking?' Triumphantly he split the money into four shares and handed them their contributions. Eddie saw that the bus was approaching his stop. He ran quickly down the steps.

Dave said, 'You didn't have to tell him we got the loot back. That way, we could've had his share, see?'

Some three weeks later they sat in the public bar of their favourite pub, but with one noticeable difference: they were only three in number.

'Rotten thing to happen,' Bob observed for the fourth time. 'Never thought he would have ended up like that.'

Peter nodded glumly. 'He could handle a bike like no one else I ever saw.' He gulped down a large helping of his lager. 'You been to see him since he came home?'

Bob turned the corners of his mouth down. 'Yeah. He's still the same: his mother told me the doctors say he'll be in that wheelchair all his life.'

Eddie contributed: 'I couldn't get any sense out of him. About how it happened, I mean. All he said was, "It came at me from nowhere." Over and over he said it.'

Bob shrugged. 'One thing – it was his own bike, not one he'd nicked. So he gets a fair bit off the insurance, you know? His mother says he'll get a cheque regular every week.'

Eddie put down his glass. 'That's funny.'

'Funny, is it?'

'No, I mean funny peculiar. We were talking, couple of days before he got smashed up, about the night we went out to see that old fraud in Crestwood, and I asked him what he'd thought of – what he wanted to do, like. I remembered just now that he laughed and said he hadn't believed in it and all he'd thought was, he'd like to just have a good bit of money regular without working.'

Bob looked puzzled. 'What about it? Oh, I see what you mean. Yeah, it came true all right, poor bastard. Funny coincidence.'

'What did you think of, when he told us to concentrate?' Eddie asked Peter.

'Oh . . . swimming. I couldn't think of anything else.'

Bob laughed sourly. 'You can't earn your living from that.'

'You can if you're good enough. Get up to championship

64

standard, see, Olympics and that, then you get the advertising, and then become a coach.'

He was very good at swimming, Eddie knew: had represented his school more than once, in fact. Eddie privately thought it an impractical choice but he said nothing: at least it had been more definite than his own indecisive plans.

Peter shivered suddenly and looked round. 'This is a damned cold place. Let's go down to the Grapes. They might have a fire on in there.'

Exactly a fortnight after this conversation, Eddie came out of the post office near his home and saw Bob walking slowly on the crowded pavement on the other side of the street. Eddie made to cross over, hesitated, then went a few yards along to a pedestrian crossing. Six weeks ago, he would have thought nothing of weaving through the traffic, but of late he had begun to avoid risks of any kind.

Once across, he caught up with his friend and tapped him on the shoulder. To his astonishment Bob spun round with a cry and fell back against a shop window. After a few seconds his staring eyes recognized Eddie. He pulled himself upright and the colour began to return to his face.

'What d'you want to do that for?'

Eddie stared at him. Bob could never have been described as intellectually brilliant, but Eddie had never known him to show fear.

'Well, I'm sorry, mate. I didn't mean to—'

'Have you heard about Peter?' Bob interrupted.

'Eh? Peter? What?'

'It was on the local radio this morning. They were talking about it in the betting shop just now, too.' Bob jerked a thumb at that establishment. 'He was coming back from the swimming baths last night – you know there's a short cut over the common? Well, he went and fell over the edge of the old reservoir there. They found him this morning.'

Eddie knew the disused reservoir. Its slippery sides and cold dead water had taken the lives of two or three small children over the last few years. He said incredulously: 'But Peter can swim – could, I mean. And there's a huge great wire fence all round it. He *couldn't* have fallen in.'

'He did, though,' said Bob grimly. 'There was a big section of the fence missing, torn down. He must have gone through it in the dark, and once he was in he couldn't get out. They say he must have been swimming round for ages before he – well.'

'Here – isn't that what he said he'd asked for that night?'

'Asked for? What d'you mean? What you looking like that for?'

Eddie's voice rose shrilly, and several passers-by glanced at them curiously. 'Don't you see? It's Robbins that's doing it. Dave got what he'd wanted, only not the way he wanted it; now Peter. He wanted to make a living from swimming, and he ended up swimming for his life!'

Bob looked slowly around him, at the shop-fronts and the passing crowd. A bus groaned past; two policemen moved calmly along the pavement opposite. He shook his head doubtfully. 'He couldn't do that, could he?'

'You don't know what he might be able to do,' said Eddie darkly. 'But I'll tell you one thing – when you asked him how much it would be, he came up with exactly the sum we'd brought. How did he do that?'

Bob stared. 'That's right! I remember it set me back at the time. I thought it was just a coincidence.'

'Too many coincidences. Something else: Dave told me that when he said to Robbins he'd seen someone in the garden, it was true – but he told me he was never quite sure what it was.'

'Perhaps it was a dog,' Bob suggested unhappily. 'Matter of fact, he told me about it on the way home that night, but I never paid much attention.'

Eddie considered telling him something of what he had been reading recently in the reference section of the public library, but decided against it. Instead he said, 'Look, we'd better give him the money back.'

Bob would have none of this. Robbins might have somehow caused Dave's crash and Peter's death, he declared, but he, Bob, would not be so easy a target. 'For two pins I'd go out there and knife the old bastard,' he spat. 'That'd settle him.'

'You got a suspended sentence last time you cut somebody,' Eddie reminded him.

Bob swore. The old man lived alone, he said: it would be easy to get in at the rear of the house undetected and out again.

'I'm going to take my share back, anyway,' said Eddie. 'I'm not going to chance finishing up in a wheelchair, or dead.'

He began to walk away, then turned back. 'What did *you* think of, in that room when he was doing all that mumbo-jumbo?'

Bob shrugged. 'If you must know, I had it in my mind that a government job would be best – it's permanent, like. Don't see how he can twist that like he did the others, eh?' He looked round suddenly. 'Bloody horrible laugh some people have got.'

Eddie's parents were still out at work when he returned home. He spent the rest of the afternoon reading some of the books he had borrowed from the non-fiction section of the library: thick volumes on witchcraft, black magic, Satanism, and the voodoo cult of Haiti. He sat in the gathering dusk for a long time, considering what he had read and trying to relate some of it to what had happened in Mr Robbins' house.

Could he use the same unearthly powers himself, he wondered, to somehow destroy Robbins? Even if he could – and it would mean obtaining many strange and unusual substances – he could never master the art in a short time. And time, he was acutely aware, was the one thing he did not have.

At last he rose, stretched, and went to the window. Outside, the moonlight had turned the lawn to silver, and clear sharp shadows lay on it. He stiffened. What was it that cast that shadow? A bush? A man?

Not a bush, certainly, for it moved forward. Eddie glimpsed a pair of ruby-red eyes that glared up at his window, and sprang back with a cry. The pile of books behind him went over with a crash.

He heard a quick soft padding on the landing outside the door, and his heart lurched and hammered. Was this what had sprung from out of nowhere at Dave, and sent his machine swerving to disaster? And torn down the wire fence at the reservoir? He waited breathlessly and watched the door.

Something brushed against it on the other side, and there was a faint tapping. His mind teetered on the edge of hysteria, and as though from a long way off he heard his mother's voice: 'Are you all right, Eddie? Was it you that called out?'

Eddie choked out some reply. The deathly chill that had gripped him drained away.

His share of the money was still in his jacket pocket: next day he went out to Crestwood and approached Robbins' house. When he was half-way up the neatly kept gravel path, the front door opened and Mr Robbins stood looking at him. Eddie stopped and held up the banknotes.

'I've – I've brought you some of the money back. I didn't know they'd taken it, honest.'

The man in the doorway laughed shortly. 'I know that. You fool! Do you think I care who took it?' He began to close the door.

'No – wait! Can't you call it quits? We won't bother you again if you leave us alone.'

Mr Robbins said venomously: 'Even if I wanted to save you I could not. You are not unintelligent: you well know that once set in motion, a great force cannot be stopped.'

Sick at heart, Eddie made his way back home. There was a police station near the bus stop, and he paused irresolutely outside it. But what could he tell these down-to-earth men in blue, and how could they help him? He went on, passing a modern red-brick church: Here, too, he could envisage no help.

Bob was not in the Black Bull, and neither was he in the Grapes. Eddie found himself unusually ill at ease in the crowded bar. He made his way home, using the well-lit main roads instead of the shorter route through dark avenues.

His parents were sitting staring blankly at the television screen. Eddie sat down and put his head in his hands. The newsreader said something about Crestwood; Eddie looked up sharply. His father grunted impatiently and pressed the channel selector button. Tiny footballers ran on a vivid green pitch.

'Hey!' Eddie protested. 'I was watching that.'

'The news? Oh, very well.' Mr Good switched the set back irritably. The newsreader's face had been replaced by a filmed report. A man holding a microphone was standing at a garden gate;

behind him could be seen the front of a house. Eddie recognized it immediately. It was the home of Mr Robbins.

The reporter said with the customary artificial urgency: 'The dead man was found lying just inside the front door. Neighbours and passers-by, alerted by his cries, forced an entry. It is understood that two of them have been admitted to hospital and are being treated for shock. A police spokesman confirmed a few minutes ago that a man had been observed climbing over the back wall of the garden. He was apprehended by two officers and is to be charged with carrying an offensive weapon.'

Mr Good switched channels again. Eddie got up slowly and took the crumpled bundle of notes from his pocket. He placed them on the coffee table.

'I . . . won't need this now,' he said absently. 'Goodnight.'

Eight months later, Eddie stood at the bar of the Grapes and read once more the account in a daily paper of Bob's conviction. The case had aroused wide interest, perhaps because of the ferocity of the attack. A reaction was sweeping the country against violent crime, and this mood had been reflected in the sentence. Bob would spend virtually all his life in Fairhill, a recently opened prison that had already earned a fearsome reputation. Four prisoners there had committed suicide. Bob had got what he had asked for that evening last year, Eddie told himself: he was working for the government – and he had been right, it was indeed permanent. Eddie laid the paper aside and called for another drink. His reflected image smiled at him in the mirror behind the bar: he was putting on weight, he noticed.

His thoughts became smug and comforting. Robbins is dead and buried – he can't touch me now.

He took his drink across to a table near the fire, for it was chilly in the pub.

He had come out of the affair quite well, he mused. If nothing else, I've learned the possibility of using the Black Arts. Why, there's no reason why I shouldn't try to discover more.

Eleven years after this momentous idea occurred to him, his parents died in a car crash; there is no suggestion that this sad event was anything other than accidental. Their son, now grown sleek and self-assured, looked for a better dwelling than their council house. He was not really surprised when an estate agent offered him the address of Mr Robbins' house. The present owners, it seemed, were willing to sell at a low price to obtain a quick sale.

'Really,' the agent confided to his client, 'to be quite honest with you, this property has been through three or four hands in the last few years. I can't imagine why.'

Shortly after moving there, Mr Edward Good went to the door in answer to a ring at the bell, and found a thin-faced youth standing on the path.

'You Mr Good?' The caller looked vaguely surprised. 'I – I phoned this morning. Somebody told me you can sometimes help people with—' He blushed furiously. 'There's this girl at work . . .'

Mr Good held open the door and beamed encouragingly. 'Please – come inside. I am sure I will be delighted to help you.'

Closing the door as his visitor entered, he added silently: 'At a price, of course, at a price.'

Outside in the garden something with glowing red eyes swung its head to stare at the door.

# Alan W. Lear

# Let's do something naughty

'You just run and play in the garden, Tracy darling. Mummy's got to get ready for her lover to come and screw her.'

My God, Pat Ashover realized as her seven-year-old daughter skipped chubbily across the lawn, for two pins I'd have said it, too. What's the matter with me?

The garden was a summer's fantasy of colour, loud with the song of linnets and thrushes, goldcrests and collared doves. It was a perfect setting for the house, whose pink distempered, pebble-dashed walls and red-tiled, crazily gabled and turreted roof turned it into something out of a fairy-tale, a gingerbread confection.

Everything around me is bright, everything is innocent. Why am I trying to make it dirty?

The house was leased for the summer. Every morning, Paul drove the twenty miles to Edinburgh to spend the day poring over mouldering trial transcripts in the National Library of Scotland. He was preparing a documentary series for the BBC, and he it was who had chosen this house when they decided to come to Scotland. The chance of living under the same roof that had once housed the unspeakable Robert Bell and his sister Grizel was just too good to miss.

'What line of work's your husband in, Pat?'

'Oh, he's a leading authority seventeenth-century British witchcraft.'

'Really? He must be an interesting chap to know.'

Fascinating. That is, if you happen to like little balding perfect gentlemen in tweed jackets and hand-knitted sweaters, who drink a cup of Ovaltine every evening and make love to their wives on the first Monday of each month, taking never less than twelve and never more than sixteen minutes over it. If you liked milk-and-water, safe-as-houses, terribly terribly nice crashing bores.

Tracy was Paul's daughter all right. Watching her skip down to the elms at the bottom of the garden, Pat Ashover experienced an irrational wave of anger against the little girl. Why must she always be so clean? Look at her – spotless pink pinafore, gleaming white sun-hat. Why can't she get dirty? At her age, I'd have been black as the ace of spades before I got halfway across the lawn. I'd like to find a patch of mud somewhere and roll the little prig in it until she . . . No, I wouldn't. No I wouldn't no I wouldn't no I wouldn't!

Shaking her auburn head in confusion, Pat closed the door and made her way upstairs. They were narrow stairs, crooked and uneven, so that it was easy to trip on them if you'd overdone the brandy after dinner. Most of the house had yielded to the passionate advances of the modernization-happy owners, but the staircase still remained uncompromisingly seventeenth-century. Robert and Grizel Bell would have felt completely at home on it.

In the bedroom, Pat started to undress. Callum would arrive at any minute, and she didn't want him to see her as she was, in her uniform, the frowsty chains of an unfulfilled housewife and mother.

Why do I have these feelings about Tracy? It's not natural. Do I resent her because she reminds me I'm no longer a teenager? Heavens, I must be the only mother in the world who gets angry with her daughter for not being naughty.

She screwed up her checked shirt and patched corduroys and flung them disdainfully into the corner. Standing before the wardrobe mirror she pulled in her stomach and threw back her shoulders to make her full breasts stand out. A grin came to her face.

Naughty . . . It was the mother, not the daughter, who was guilty of naughtiness. The things she and Callum got up to while Paul was away – adventurous, inventive, perverse things, often weird and occasionally downright painful . . .

That trick last week left me with bruises all over a very awkward place. I don't know how I'd have explained them if Paul had noticed . . . but of course, Paul wouldn't, would he?

No, the most exciting time you ever had with Paul was when he sat in front of the big living-room fireplace in the evenings, chuckling to himself and reading out the juicier bits of the trials he'd studied that day. In particular, the accounts of the 'lewd and lascivious practices' of the Reverend Robert Bell and his sister

Grizel, burned together at the stake in the city of Edinburgh on the 25th July, 1670, would have made anybody's hair curl.

'Oh, our Robbie Bell was a right lad,' Paul had declared. 'He was a real hellfire preacher for forty years at the church in the village down the road from here. People used to come from miles around to hear him, and they invited him to do guest spots in half the churches in Edinburgh. He was about as popular in his day as Barry Manilow. Merchants of the city used to invite him to come to their house and pray with their women-folk, behind locked doors. That was the subject of much furore after what happened, I can tell you.

'One day Robbie gets the chance of a lifetime: to speak from the pulpit of the High Kirk of St Giles. There's a packed house, of course, all ready to have the fear of God put into them. Women are swooning before he even speaks. So he climbs up, looks out over the congregation, and then he starts. Oh yes, he starts all right.

'Tells them he's a black witch who sold his soul to Satan forty years before. Ever since then, he and his sister have been sacrificing to hell every week and have been guilty in their time of more sexual abominations than the congregation had ever heard of. Bestiality, necrophilia, sadism, incest of course . . .' Paul's round, pink face was turning moist. 'Paedophilia with their little niece, sodomy with boys from the church choir, a little dismemberment here and there, human sacrifice, disembowelling, cannibalism . . . his speciality seems to have been raping women to death in the village church.'

'What, all by himself?'

'Old Robert claimed Satan had given him the power to copulate for hours on end without ceasing. His sister confirmed that, as indeed she confirmed all his other confessions.' Paul giggled. 'Hours on end . . . a talent many men might envy, eh?'

'Pity he's not around now,' Pat had replied.

Was it any wonder I ended up letting myself get laid by the village handyman? she thought angrily now, throwing a white silk gown about her shoulders and beginning to brush out her hair.

Callum wasn't much – semi-literate, none too clean, a bit too fond of the rough stuff for her liking – but at least he could give her what she needed for an hour or so every day.

Mind you, there were some ideas of his that she just couldn't bring herself to like . . .

Like the way he insisted on making love to her in the nursery, on little Tracy's bed. He claimed that the master bedroom stank of Paul and put him off, but Pat knew there was more to it than that.

The nursery, in spite of every attempt to render it bright and modern, remained the most seventeenth-century room in the house. The sloping ceiling, mullioned window and Jacobean stonework showing through the Bugs Bunny wallpaper invested all the little girl's possessions with a dark, sinister aura. Instead of cute home-liness, there was something unwholesome about the fluffy animals in the corner, the plastic dollies outside their dolls' house, the narrow bed with gingerbread men on the quilt, the Lego scattered by the wall.

But Callum said the room turned him on. And Pat, afraid he might leave her to her frustration if she balked at anything he suggested, let him take her again and again on the child's bed, on the floor among the dolls or astride the big wooden rocking-horse. Of all the perversions they had encompassed together, this was the one that troubled Pat's conscience the most: that her daughter slept every night amongst the memories of her mother's filth.

Oh, so what? It wouldn't do her any harm to get a load of what the real world's like.

She tore the bedroom curtains open and sat in the window, so she'd see Callum's van the moment it came up the drive. Maybe she didn't like all the things they did together, but he was necessary to her. Looking out, she caught sight of Tracy underneath the elms at the bottom of the garden. There was a little boy with her: one of the local children, a year or so older than the girl, wearing shorts and a Darth Vader t-shirt.

Pat had seen him before, and chaffed Tracy about having a boyfriend. They didn't seem to be having a very jolly game just now: they were standing quite still in the shadow of a tree, talking earnestly together.

He's probably asking her to show him what she's got. Well, why not? You go ahead, Tracy love. Complete your education.

It must be over a quarter of a century, Pat realized, since she had gone behind the bicycle sheds at school with little – what was his name? – Johnny Redgate. He'd dropped his khaki shorts for her inspection, and she'd fulfilled her part of the bargain by dropping

74

her navy blues while he gawped at her. So long ago!

And now the next generation was *vive*-ing the same *difference*, eh? Well, good luck to them!

A cloud passed in front of the sun.

Its shadow, falling on the window, turned it for a moment into a mirror in which Pat could see her face. Only it wasn't her face. It was a grinning demon, a shameless, lecherous hag sitting naked in a thin white robe, her face flushed and her eyes burning with the vile, lubricious thoughts behind them.

My God! Is that me? What's the matter with me?

For a moment she sat as though petrified. Then the hairbrush dropped to the floor as she buried her face in her hands.

I'm not like that! I'm not! And Tracy's not like that either!

Tracy, who was modest to the point of absurdity. Tracy, who wouldn't undress if her parents were in the room, who insisted on bathing behind locked doors, in spite of Pat's fear of accidents.

It's unimaginable that she'd do anything wicked like that. And yet I keep imagining it. I can't even look at her without thinking filth – I can't look at anything at all without turning it into something obscene. Everything I see, every word I hear becomes a dirty joke. Like a teenage nymphomaniac – but I'm no teenager, and I've never had any problems like that before. Oh God, what am I turning into?

Night after night she spent tossing and turning next to her plump, softly breathing husband. She hadn't had a decent night's sleep for months: she lay for hours on end, burning up with desire, visualizing over and over again scenes of depravity and evil, an endless series of atrocious orgies in which she was violated in ever more unclean, ever more hellish ways.

And by day, wandering through the house, her thoughts kept returning to the abominations that Robert and Grizel Bell had committed, two hundred years before, beneath this crooked, multi-dimensional roof.

I was never like that before. Never. Not until we moved into this house. It's as if someone else was inside me, possessing me, taking me over . . .

The sun came out again. Slowly Pat raised her head. At last, at long last, her mind had enunciated the thought that had been struggling within her for birth ever since this summer had begun.

'Grizel Bell,' Pat whispered, trembling all over, 'Is that you? Are you in me?'

They hadn't been afraid when they mounted the scaffold in 1670. Flames and death had not daunted them, the contemporary accounts insisted. 'We go,' Robert Bell had declared to his warders, 'but tae change these auld and spavinned bodies for new anes and fresh, wherein we may sate oor hellish lusts for all eternity the-gither.'

And Grizel, when the soldiers came to arrest her, had looked back at this house and called, 'I leave thee not, me bonny hame. Thy roof shall always be a shelter for the soul of Grizel Bell.'

Pat began to weep. She knew it all now. That rotten soul was in her, using her body as a mere vehicle in which to plumb the depths of depravity and sickness, sinking lower and lower every time Callum came to the house and—

The sudden noise of a heavy van rounding the corner and starting up the gravel drive. Pat let out a breathless scream.

Callum . . . They said they would be together. If Grizel Bell lives on inside me, then Callum . . . Callum who seems so slow, so lacking in imagination, but whose mind comes up with sexual elaborations the like of which I'd never have believed . . .

Is the spirit of Robert Bell outside, approaching my door to take me in my little daughter's bed?

Underneath the elms, Tracy Ashover and the little boy in the Darth Vader t-shirt watched the battered green Morris van toil up the steep driveway and clank to a halt in front of the white-painted front door. A man got out and strode up to knock. He was about twenty, swarthy and tanned, not tall but very broadly built. There was a grin on his fleshy, low-browed face: an animal grin showing uneven, very white teeth. He wore jeans and a black leather jacket with a lion rampant on the back. He knocked on the door far harder than was necessary.

The children saw Tracy's mother appear, in her sheer silk robe and fluffy mules. There was fear on her pale face, and for a moment she tried to say something to the man; but he only shouldered past her and closed the door. A minute or so later, the curtains were drawn in the nursery upstairs.

A blackbird began to sing in a nearby elm. There was a rustling in the long grass as a squirrel passed. The children resumed their conversation. They began as they talked to move out of the little copse, and up the lawn towards the house with its crow-stepped gables and curiously angled roof. They talked gravely, quietly. A white butterfly passed close by their heads, but they didn't turn to look . . .

I won't scream. I'll keep calm. I've done what I had to do, and now there are other things to be done, other things to think of . . .

The light in the nursery was yellow, sunlight diffused through Goldilocks curtains. In the middle of the floor stood the big wooden rocking-horse. Paul hadn't been too happy for Tracy to have a rocking-horse as big as that; he was afraid she might fall off and strike her head. But she hardly ever played on it, so it was all right.

Callum was slumped across the horse's back. He was wearing nothing but his underpants. They were garish underpants, showing a design of a bantam wearing boxing gloves with the legend 'Super Cock'. They were so badly stained and faded that it was hardly discernible. The horse rolled back and forward under him, increasingly slowly, and his limp hands brushed the floor in time to the rhythm.

On the other side of the horse lay a half-built edifice of Lego bricks. White bricks, yellow, blue and red, and little Lego men amongst them with buttons for eyes. Mixed in with the bricks was a mortar of blood, black hairs, and grey and white blobs of brain.

Pat let the clotted money-box drop from her hand. It was a sturdy affair of tin and hard plastic, shaped like a clown, and it was heavy with the coins Tracy had saved. Tracy was a thrifty girl. Pat wiped her hands carefully on the skirt of a black baby doll, and used the same cloth for the blood which had sprayed her naked body.

I'm safe now. I've got rid of Robert Bell. And they said they'd always be together, didn't they? So Grizel must have gone as well. Right. So everything's fine, isn't it? There's no need to scream.

Now what does Pat have to do? Right. She has to get rid of Callum's body. Then she has to clean up the nursery, so no one will know what's happened. Now, on with thinking caps. You can put him in his van, drive him into the woods and set his van on fire. That's good.

But how am I going to get the body to the van? That heavy weight.

How am I even going to get him down the stairs without leaving traces behind?

Don't scream! Think!

He's too big, too heavy. Well, what do you do with something that's too heavy?

Pat's ashen face slowly worked itself into something like a smile. She picked the white silk robe from Tracy's bed and wrapped herself in it, slipping her feet into the mules at the same time.

Of course. You make it lighter. Now, what am I going to need?

Big black plastic bags. There are plenty in the kitchen. And what else is in the kitchen, eh Pat?

The meat-axe . . .

She was almost singing as she left the nursery and made her way down the twisted stairs. Almost enjoying herself. A few minutes ago the world had been full of terror, but now . . .

Tracy and the little boy in the Darth Vader t-shirt stood together, grave and thoughtful at the foot of the stairs.

'What are you doing here?' Pat screamed at them. 'Get back in the garden at once!'

The children stood their ground.

'We're fed up with the garden,' Tracy said.

'That's right,' said the boy. He spoke with a pronounced local accent.

'We want to play in the nursery,' said Tracy.

Pat's head began to swim dangerously.

'You can't.'

'Why not?' Tracy asked.

Pat was taken aback by the expression in the little girl's eyes. In a grown-up, it would have signified someone hard and determined, someone it wouldn't be wise to cross. The eyes were glittering icily, and Pat felt suddenly vulnerable, as though they were penetrating her silk robe to the soft nakedness beneath.

The boy's eyes held an identical gleam.

'We want to play in the nursery,' he repeated.

'Well, you can't! That's final! Now get out of here at once before I give you both a good hiding!'

That's what she should have said – that's what she wanted to say – but she didn't. Suddenly there was no strength left in her; reaction to the horror and violence upstairs set in all at once and she sank down on to the bottom step, her head sagging.

'Please,' she muttered weakly, 'Please don't go up there. For Mummy's sake. Please.'

Tracy turned to the little boy. There followed a moment's wordless communication.

'Will you play with us down here if we agree not to go up there?' she asked at last.

Pat felt too drained to argue. 'All right. But it'll have to be a quick game, because Mummy's got something she has to do before Daddy comes home.'

The children considered the acceptability of this.

'OK,' the boy said at last. 'Let's play at redskins.'

Tracy's face lit up. She began to skip from one foot to the other in excitement. 'Smashing! You can be our prisoner, Mummy.'

'Come on.' The boy grabbed Pat's limp hand and pulled her roughly up from the step. She let herself be dragged from the hallway into the cavernous stone kitchen. Her mind raced.

It's only half past eleven. We'll have this game, then I'll give them lunch, then they'll go and leave me in peace. Tracy won't disobey. She's just showing off in front of her little friend now, but Tracy's not a naughty girl.

Paul won't be home till six at the earliest. There's plenty of time. I've nothing at all to be worried about.

Wish I had more clothes on, though. I shouldn't be like this in front of children – naked under my robe. It's not decent.

'Sit down here, paleface,' Tracy ordered, letting out a warwhoop.

The boy tugged Pat's arm and she half-fell into a wide-bottomed wooden kitchen chair. He really was strong for his age, this freckled toe-rag in the Darth Vader t-shirt.

'Fetchum rope,' he ordered Tracy.

A few moments later, while the little girl danced around them with blood-curdling screams, Pat submitted to having her hands tied behind her.

'Ow!' she protested as the strong kitchen cord bit her wrists. 'Not so tight, sonny.'

'Paleface not talk,' the boy commanded.

'Did you learn to tie knots like that in the Cubs?' Pat asked. The boy knelt in front of her.

'Now legs.' He gripped Pat's right ankle and began to tie it to the leg of the heavy wooden chair.

Pat had a moment of panic. Suppose they tied her to the chair so she couldn't move, then ran off and left her? At six o'clock she'd be found, helpless in the kitchen, with that *thing* in the nursery still slumped there, evidence to send her away forever . . .

Real horror began to creep into her mind. Supposing they left her alone, tied to this chair . . . Supposing Callum began to stir, to haul himself off the wooden rocking-horse, and then with slow, deliberate, dragging footsteps to descend the stairs while she could do nothing but sit here screaming . . . supposing he entered the kitchen, with claw-like hands extended to grip her, one eye dangling on his cheek and a red, curdled hole where half of his face ought to be . . .

The little boy pulled her left leg roughly to the other side of the chair and began to bind it. Pat came out of her daze with a gasp of surprise. The chair really was uncomfortably wide; her legs were as far apart as they could go, as far apart as they'd ever been since she gave birth to Tracy. It was a most unpleasant feeling. The front of her robe no longer overlapped all the way down, and the inside of her thighs were plainly visible to all who cared to look.

Pat opened her mouth to protest – this certainly wasn't at all proper – but then shut it again. The children seemed to have finished their game. They were standing in front of her now, silent and motionless, and the smiles on their faces were no longer the smiles of children.

'Let's not play redskins any more,' said Tracy. Her voice seemed suddenly different from itself: deeper, more mature.

'No,' the boy agreed. 'Tell ye what. Let's dae something naughty.'

'Naughty?' Pat's mouth had gone dry. 'What do you mean, naughty?'

'*You* know, Mummy!' Tracy said. 'You show us yours, and then we'll show you ours. Don't tell me you've never played that game before.'

'Tracy!' Pat gasped. 'How dare you suggest such a thing? Untie me this instant! Just wait till your father gets home, I'm going to tel' him all about this disgraceful episode and then you know what he'll do? He'll take—'

Tracy brought her hand from where it had been hiding behind her back.

The carving knife was in it.

Pat was struck dumb. Her eyes bulged in her face, her jaw hung open. A little drool rolled down her chin, but she didn't notice.

Tracy moved behind her. Carefully, economically, she used the razor-sharp blade to cut down the back of Pat's white silk robe. Next, moving to the front, she untied the sash and pulled the two halves away from her mother's body.

The grin on the little boy's face widened.

Pat sat bound, naked and trembling. She couldn't speak, or take her eyes off the face of the child who stood there in his Darth Vader t-shirt, contemplating her wide-open thighs. Still grinning, he began to speak.

'Bravely done, my sister. Even wi' hands as small as these, thou'st no lost thy wonted skill wi' a blade.'

That wasn't a child's voice. Nor was the voice that issued from the mouth of Tracy Ashover.

'Nor no skill ither, Robbie ma love. Have I no ettled every night tae send the daemons of lust tae harry this wench, that she suld be ready for thee when the time were right?'

'I doot she conceived 'twas Grizel Bell hersel whae lusted wi' in her,' chuckled the boy, and Tracy let out a hag's cackle.

'In *her*? What for would I choose an auld hen like thon, when this bonny bairn lay ready for the plucking? A pickle changes here an' there, and she was all I could require. But why dae we delay? The game's no done yet, is it, Mummy? Thou hast shown us thy own, now 'tis time for us tae show thee oors.'

She inserted the knife down the front of her pink pinafore dress and wrenched it forward with unnatural force. The cloth parted. A pair of woman's breasts, full and mature, fell into view. They were each bigger than the head of the little girl whose body they defiled – grotesque, blasphemous, obscene.

The boy pulled his t-shirt over his head, revealing a chest of matted black hair. Then, his chubby hands fumbling over the buttons, he pulled down his grey terylene shorts.

Booming within her head like the pounding of fists inside the lid of a coffin, Paul's voice came back to Pat.

'Old Robert claimed that Satan had given him the power to copulate for hours on end without ceasing. His speciality was raping women to death . . .'

The monster with Tracy's face began to sing.

'Come on, Mummy, close your eyes, Robbie's going to give you a big surprise . . .'

# Christina Kiplinger
# Grave business

His arms ached as he lifted the last shovelful of dry earth. The box lay before him. Anxiously patting the wood box, he lifted himself from the dark hole.

A streak of lightning lit the sky as the crane pulled the box from its place of rest. Arthur smiled. He saw how shiny the ebony wood was and it gave him a warm feeling. Thinking of her now, he remembered how lovely her embalmed face had looked. It seemed that no matter what Mr Bond did, the mortician could not do justice to the raven-haired beauty. Arthur didn't care. He had seen the beauty of her milky-white skin, had imagined the moistness of her cherry-red lips. As he lifted the ebony lid, Arthur felt a ripple of excitement pierce him.

They sat together at a small red covered table. Arthur poured wine into a goblet and placed it before her.

'I think I'll call you Betsy,' he sighed. 'You look like a Betsy.' Her large eyes, blue-grey circles, were propped open with tooth-picks Arthur kept in his pants pocket. He had worked a smile on to her slowly deteriorating face and her beauty was overbearing.

The dank mausoleum was filled with the echo of Arthur's voice.

'Sorry, dear,' he said. 'I'll try to keep it lower.' Looking at the statuesque Betsy, a small laugh escaped him. He knew that the loudness would not bother her now.

Carving the cornish hen, Arthur gave Betsy a serving and hungrily devoured his own food. Suddenly, he looked up. A glazed look overtook his warm brown eyes.

'Betsy! You're not eating your food!' he said. 'We can't waste food, can we?' His voice turned to a screech in the quiet darkness. It bellowed as it echoed from the cement walls. The corpse remained silent, staring dully ahead.

'Eat,' Arthur said with a grunt, 'How can we have a good time if you don't eat?'

As if a second thought struck him, Arthur rose. Smiling at Betsy, he walked to a battery-operated radio resting near the door. After sampling various frequencies, Arthur was finally satisfied with a dull easy listening station.

'You still have not eaten!' Arthur screamed at Betsy. The corpse sat still as it had been since Arthur had dragged it from the clear, cold evening. 'Well,' he smiled to himself, 'I guess you'll just have to make up for it in other ways.' In one swift movement, he tipped the table over and threw Betsy to the floor.

Arthur made love to her quickly and furiously, without forethought. It was over as soon as it had begun. Arthur broke into tears.

'It's always the same,' he said quietly, 'You, all of you, use me. And when it's over – you won't even talk to me!' Receiving no sympathy from the unyielding corpse, Arthur stood angrily. Throwing Betsy over his shoulder, he took her back to the dank grave.

The sun was starting to come up when Arthur finished filling in the hole. He thought angrily of what had happened to his well-planned evening. Betsy had turned it into an utter travesty. Never again! He made a vow to give up this grave business that he indulged in on clear evenings. It just wasn't worth it! Tomorrow evening would find him, Arthur Justine, in his usual capacity of security guard to Greenville Cemetery. He would spend his day as he had this day. Practising his hobby of watching Mr Bond, the mortician, embalm the dead.

As daylight filled the sky, Arthur got into his pick-up truck, safe in the knowledge of his vow. Suddenly, he remembered the flaming redhead being buried today. It was going to be a clear night, he mused, and he *did* have one cornish hen left. . .

# Alan Ryan

# Onawa

Yesterday – almost three hundred years ago now – I bit off the head of a bird.

It was a very small bird, but I dared take nothing larger at the time, hardly dared think what I was doing, even in the moment I did it. The bird was a sparrow, I think, all grey and brown, feathers the colour of dried mud near a river's edge or dead leaves turning to mulch, colours invisible against the forest floor or among the shifting shadows and branches of a tree. A bird of no consequence, a tiny, shivering, twittering thing. I thought it beautiful.

That was the first time, the beginning. There have been better times since, there are better times now – at least in some regards – and, of course, a better method of taking what I need, what I so often crave. But that time was the first: it was clumsy, inefficient, terrifying, thrilling. I can still taste the bird. Still taste it.

I called myself Onawa then.

I was eleven years old.

The forest still grows thick around the shores of Lake Otsego in upstate New York. Cooperstown is there now, named after the father of the writer. I remember the father, a big, hearty man, very much in charge of his wilderness domain, a judge meting out forest justice tempered by civilization. I remember his son too; I saw him once or twice. Today that part of the mountain country is dotted with towns and dairy farms. Then it was all forest, except for a struggling patch here and there, a narrow path through the woods, a tiny village on the edge of the lake. They were lovely forests, dark, thick, pillared with grand old trees, hushed with ageless silence, crossed only by the tracks of forest animals and the occasional flights of birds. I loved the forest.

I came from the forest.

I remember the day.

The woods had been dark, tall trees blocking the sunlight, and I vaguely remember wandering, picking my way between trees, stepping over fallen trunks, crossing a brook once or twice. Then the trees thinned out as I drew near the edge of the lake. The light grew brighter and before me I could see the glimmer of the lake, its surface shimmering in the sun like a reflecting glass. Then my bare feet touched a hard surface, stones and rocks at the water's edge, and I was standing in dazzling sunlight, blinking back dazzled tears.

I was naked.

The day was warm but a cool breeze blew across the lake, as if seeking me out in particular. It touched my belly, touched my nipples, whipped my hair so that I felt it move across my shoulders. I remember tossing my head to swing the long tickling hair from my cheek and neck. I stood there, facing out over the silent water for some while, keeping my eyes half closed, and only gradually opening them to admit no more light than they could tolerate after the darkness of the forest. The breeze continued to touch me.

And I asked myself: Who am I? And did not know. I didn't know my name or where I was or where I had been or had come from. I was like the breeze itself, I remember thinking, coming from nowhere and going maybe nowhere, maybe everywhere.

After some minutes, when the daylight no longer blinded me, I knelt at the water's edge, shiny bare knees on rough rock, and leaned forward to look at my reflection, to see who and what I was. It is so hard, I see now from this different perspective, to know oneself and yet not know oneself. People suffering amnesia must feel as I did then: knowing one is alive and well, perfectly normal, and knowing one has a history but not knowing what it is. I saw myself in the water, found myself floating there, the image shifting and blurring, then suddenly detailed as crystal, then blurred again as the breeze rippled the water. A young girl, beautiful – I knew it instinctively then, know it even better now – with a fine nose, high dramatic cheekbones, dark dark eyes, straight black hair blowing free and glossy about my face, framing it, and skin the colour of pale tea, rich and reddish-brown. But whose face? Strangely, I felt no fear at not knowing.

'Stand up there! Make no other move!'

I jumped so quickly that one of my toes, bent beneath me as I crouched, twisted against the rock and sent hot pain flashing through my foot. I yelped and had to scramble to keep my balance. When I turned toward the voice, I saw the man staring at me, at my face, at my nakedness. His own face was heavily bearded but I could see his mouth, wet and pink, open in surprise. His eyes moved over my body, flickered involuntarily over my body, my legs, my breasts just beginning to swell, then blinked and jerked away, focused on the rock at my feet. I remember noting my surprise at feeling no fear and the sudden realization that in my nakedness lay one of my strongest weapons. It frightens and confuses women, startles and awes men. It has been so ever since, and is so today. My nipples tingled with the realization and I almost smiled.

He asked me what tribe I came from, who I belonged to, and I understood his English but had no answers. He asked me other questions too that had no answers.

'What is your name?' he asked for the second time, sensing that I understood the question.

'Onawa,' I said softly, and was surprised at my voice and the name I heard myself speaking. I do not know where the name came from, or whether it had ever sounded in my head or my ears before. 'Onawa,' I said again.

'Does it have meaning?' he asked, his eyes still shifting around, looking everywhere but at my nakedness.

The words came unbidden. 'Maiden,' I said. 'Vigilant maiden.'

He was silent for a minute, then forced his eyes to my face. I think he was still afraid, perhaps that my people would come screaming from the forest and kill him for abducting their child. He need have had no fear – not of that, at least – for I have no people.

The man's name was Edward Bracknell. His wife's name was Adelaide. They took good care of me, fed me and clothed me. The woman took an almost erotic pleasure in combing my hair every day, letting the wooden comb drag through the weight of my shining black cape of hair. The man's pleasure was no doubt erotic too. He always avoided my eyes when his wife was combing my hair, but he never looked away from what she was doing, either. I do not mean that there was anything sexual here. Edward Bracknell was a devout man who read the Bible aloud every day in the morning and in the evening, whose God lurked always just behind his shoulder. He may have had to ask his God's forgiveness for the vague stirrings that troubled him when he looked at me, but never, I am sure, for a specifically sexual thought in connection with me. I was a child. Only a child. My thoughts smile at the memory. No, he and his wife cared for me well.

I had lived with them a week when he brought the first Indian to look at me.

The Indian was tall, boldly featured and strongly muscled, his head shaved clean except for a dark brush of hair down the centre of his skull. Bracknell brought him to me one afternoon as I did chores near the door of the cabin. The Indian stared at me unblinking for a long moment, silent, only staring at me, his hard face without expression. His cheeks and jaw might have been carved from the oak of the forest. Once I saw the fingers of his right hand flex open, then instantly close again into a fist. Apart from that, he did not move.

'No,' he said at last, and I can still hear his voice.

Bracknell looked quickly at him. 'Not yours, then?' he asked.

'No,' the Indian said again. His voice was husky, as if he needed to clear his throat and would not bother. Or perhaps he was unaccustomed to speaking English. Or perhaps he was afraid. Without moving his gaze from my face, he held out his left hand toward Bracknell, with the index finger extended. Then he moved his right hand and placed that index finger across the other.

'I don't understand,' Bracknell said.

The Indian glanced at him impatiently, then fiercely rapped the one finger across the other, as if he meant to chop it off.

'Oh,' Bracknell said. 'Half. A half-breed?'

'Half,' the Indian said, having found the right word in the white man's foreign tongue.

'But what tribe?'

The Indian jerked his chin away, towards the woods beyond the cabin or the hills beyond the woods. Either he did not know or would not say. He looked back at me for an instant, his black eyes boring into mine.

'Not blood of my people,' he said clearly. Abruptly, he turned and strode away.

Bracknell stared after him. Strangely calm, I stared too.

In the following weeks, Bracknell brought other Indians to the cabin. They all did the same. None of them claimed me. I was not of the blood of their people.

So Edward and Adelaide Bracknell made me their own, took in the half-breed Indian girl – they guessed my age at eleven – and treated me as their own daughter. Adelaide chose a name for me, a Christian name, as she said, Maria, pronounced in the English fashion, *Mar-eye-ah*. I have used it a number of times since then, insisting always on that pronunciation.

I was set chores to do, things to be responsible for, and I recall being glad of them. I did not play. Where would be a child's pleasure in playing if she knows she is playing? The days passed.

But often as I lay awake at night, listening to the sounds of the forest outside and sometimes the sounds of sex from across the cabin, I thought of the Indians, especially that first one who had stared so hard and so coldly at me and said that I was not blood of his people.

The word *blood* lingered in my mind.


A few weeks after the Indians stopped coming, I got sick. Adelaide put it down to what she assumed was a severe change of diet for me; I wasn't accustomed to white people's food. But in fact I was indifferent to the food she fed me. I simply felt weak and ill. Adelaide put me to bed.

On my first day in bed, I lay there looking out through the open door of the cabin. Adelaide took one of the few precious chickens they possessed and killed it to make a healing broth. I watched her through the open doorway. She carried the chicken to the edge of the clearing, laid its neck across the stump of a tree, and with one sharp slicing movement of her wrist and arm, struck its head off with an axe. Quickly, she lifted the chicken high and let the blood drain from its jerking, headless body. It spurted out, bright red arcs of blood catching the sunlight while the body continued to spasm.

I watched the blood, fascinated. Later, when Adelaide brought me the broth and fed it to me from a wooden spoon, I thought I could taste the blood itself, the flavour lingering beneath that of the meat and salt and spices. The thought of blood might have sickened another child, even another half-breed frontier child. It did not sicken me.

But whatever had made me ill continued to do so. I lay abed for another week, Adelaide spending more and more time at my side. She prayed often and kept reading to me from the Bible. While her voice droned on – I think she was reciting more than actually reading – I thought about the blood of the chicken and found that my heart was beating faster. I liked thinking about blood.

Then one morning Edward Bracknell studied the sky and told Adelaide that the first big snow of the winter would be coming soon. He needed her help. Adelaide propped me up in the bed, made certain I was comfortable, then left me to go with him.

I felt a little stronger that day and after a while pushed myself up and sat on the edge of the bed. The cabin door was closed to keep out the cold weather. I longed to be outside, so I made my way across the floor and opened the door. The air was clear and sharp. A breeze rustled my nightgown around me, pushed it in with the force of a hand between my legs.

I had no word for what I needed, had no word for what I was, but instinct is a sure teacher. I pulled my nightgown off and stood naked in the doorway, letting the breeze – I knew it was cold but it didn't seem so to me – play about my body, feeling its touch without its chill. I felt my nipples stiffen.

Then I was running.

Barefoot, I ran across the open space in front of the cabin, ran into the woods, flung myself, hair flying, between the trees, over fallen trunks, splashed through the lovely coldness of a tiny stream that rippled over white rocks, felt branches snatch hungrily at my floating hair and kiss my face as I ran.

When finally I came to a halt, I was standing in a small clear space near the shore of the lake. The water was grey and flat beneath the overcast sky. I was laughing with the pleasure of being outside, in the woods from which I had come, and the pleasure of running naked, my body touched by breezes. My mouth was open, laughing. I felt, without pain, the cold air touch the wetness of my mouth.

Out of the corner of my eye, I saw the movement at the foot of a

90

tree. Something fluttered among the gnarled and tangled roots that crept like twisted snakes around the base of the trunk. Something small. I stepped closer to it and bent, hands on naked knees, to see what it was.

It was a bird. It was flopping among the twigs and leaves and roots. One wing beat furiously for a moment, then was still, then started beating again. The other wing did not move at all. Broken. I could see the bird's chest moving rapidly with the effort of trying to right itself and fly. Again the wing flapped, beat frantically for a minute, then stopped.

I leaned closer and stretched my hand out towards it. My fingers closed gently around its tiny, shivering body. I could feel its heart beating against my hand. I was careful not to squeeze too hard, careful not to crush it.

I held its head trapped between my thumb and index finger. Black beads of eyes jerked back and forth. The head swiveled about and the body shivered in my hand. I could feel the one good wing trying to flutter.

I brought the bird near my eyes to examine it closely, but all I could think about was the feel of its heart beating in my hand, beating, pumping blood. Pumping blood, right here in my hand. I thought of the chicken Adelaide had killed, thought of its blood spurting from the severed neck, spurting and spraying, and closed my hand a little tighter around the shivering body I held, closed it tighter to feel the heart beating, pumping, pumping.

*Not blood of my people*, I heard the Indian say.

Half-breed.

Blood. Blood of the children.

Blood of the bird, of *this* bird, of this heart beating in my hand, pumping in my hand.

Even without the words for what I was and what I needed, I wanted the blood, wanted the bird's blood.

A part of me – ever the half-breed – was terrified, but not frightened of the act itself, not repulsed, I understand now, but just frightened, the way one is frightened before the first sex, frightened but thrilled, frightened but glad, frightened but relieved. The other part of me was thinking how best to get the blood. Thus weds instinct with reason. I have seen it happen often in the centuries since.

I could not cut into the bird because I had nothing to cut with. And a cut would draw little blood anyway, it seemed. There would be little enough in the bird to begin with. How, then?

I saw in my mind the blood spraying from the head of the chicken, its heart still beating, not knowing it was dead. Its heart still beating while its head was gone.

In my hand I felt the bird's heart beating.

I kissed the top of its trembling head before I did it.

I opened my mouth. I closed my lips around the bird's head, felt with my lips for the jointure of head and body, then place where the vessel carrying the blood to the brain was most accessible. I had to guess, no way to be certain. I felt feathers in my mouth, felt the thing's beak move against my tongue, trying to peck. All this in a second.

I drew my lips apart, pulled them back from my teeth, felt again the coldness of the air against their wetness, felt the stretch and strength of my jaws, and snapped my teeth together. Crushed through feathers, sliced through skin, muscles, tendons, blood vessels. Tasted the blood. Tasted its brief warmth.

The head fell aside and filled the inside of my cheek, the tiny beak a thrilling sharpness against the soft inner skin of my mouth. Blood pulsed from the neck.

It was over in a minute. There was not much blood, but oh, it was good, it was so good.

I may have lived before that – I still do not know – but truly I was born in that minute.

When I was certain there was no more blood, I threw the drained body into the woods and spat out the head at the foot of the tree.

Later I would need more blood, and more than the blood of birds and beasts. Human blood would feed me, thrill me and feed me.

But the bird was the first.

And I can still taste it.

Ian C. Straghan

# The architect's story

'This scar on the back of my hand that you asked me about earlier on
– I've been wondering if I shouldn't give you the real story of how I
came by it. A lot of people ask me about it, and I've rather fallen into
the habit of brushing them off with some matter-of-fact explana-
tion, as I did you. But that is not really the way it happened.

'Late? Yes, you're right. The evening seems to have fairly flown
past. I daresay it's because I'm not used to having company. And
you're tired, I can see that. You've had a long day of it, travelling
down here. We didn't mind how long we sat up, talking, when we
were at Oxford, did we? Eh, well, we are both getting old, I expect.

'Tell you what, George – just reach back behind your chair and
open that cupboard, will you. You'll find a small book in there, I
fancy: a black notebook. Got it? Yes that's the one. Take it up to bed
with you, if you like. In there is the true story of this mark on my
hand. For what it is worth, you will be the first person to read it.
And if you find it boring you can lay it aside and go to sleep. *I* shan't
mind, I promise you.

'Another drink? No? Lord, listen to that wind howl outside!
You'll be snug enough in the spare room, though: Mrs Wilmott laid
a fire in there this morning, and banked it up before she went home.

'Do you know, it's something like thirty-eight years since I wrote
it all down in that book. The doctors suggested I do it, when I was
discharged from the hospital in Boarwood. Cathartic therapy or
some such name they called it. Mind you, they were right, and I did
feel better for spilling it all down on paper. I'd had some bad nights
while I was in there.

'I'll let you get off to your bed, then. Me? No, I'll sit up by the fire
a little longer, I think.

'You'll be able to find your room all right? Goodnight then,
George. Oh, here, don't forget the notebook. Goodnight.'

\*

October, 1951. I was sent down to Boarwood by my firm to sort out some error that had been made by the son of the elder partner. The site was about three miles outside Boarwood, a four-acre development we'd thought would be a straightforward job but which turned out to be more trouble, one way and another, than any we'd had before or since.

I say we, but in fact I am a very junior member of Stewart and Collins. Still, even a half-qualified junior like me could not do a worse job than young Collins had, and when the builders began to create about the slip-up, I was despatched to Boarwood. I was even given the use of the manager's car, since Boarwood had no station.

I booked in at the Stag's Head and then drove out to the building site in the fading afternoon light. Parking on the verge near the entrance, I changed my shoes for wellingtons and then stood for a moment beside the car, studying the scene.

There had originally been two fields here, and indeed the hedge still existed on three sides, while a wood fringed the fourth. That was the side nearest the town below. I knew there had also been a house on the property, but it came as a surprise to find it still standing. It was marked off from the field by a thick hedge, so that I could only see the first and top floors, and the gabled roof.

There was a small wooden hut not far inside the site, and I squelched my way over to it. Inside I found the supervisor, a little Scot called MacFadyen. He was standing at a long bench which ran the length of the shed and which was covered with delivery notes, plans, schedules, and a hundred other kinds of paperwork. His only reaction to my polite enquiry was to jerk a thumb at a sack below the bench. In it were the instruments and plans that young Collins had left. I drew them out and uttered an exclamation of annoyance. They were useless; caked in mud, rusting, and in some cases broken. The papers were damp and stained.

MacFadyen glanced down at me as I squatted beside them, swearing. I rose, with remonstrations on my lips, but he shook his head. 'That's none o' mah doin',' he said coolly. 'Yon wee man frae your firm left them lyin' in the field when he went back tae London. All Ah did wis tae fetch them in and pit them in the sack.'

It was obvious that I could do nothing until new instruments were sent down, and duplicate sheets. MacFadyen let me use the phone in the hut, and I was able to catch Turner, my boss, just before he left the office.

Before returning to the car I asked MacFadyen about the house near the road. He shook his head without interest. 'Cannae touch it till the solicitors give my gaffers the OK. Some difficulty over the deeds, Ah understand.'

'Difficulty?'

'They cannae trace the last owner, or something.'

Further questions only made him impatient. 'None o' mah concern. Yon old fellow across the road in the wee cottage wid tell ye more.' He slid open the window and bawled instructions at a lorry that was slithering past.

Reaching the car, I looked across the busy trunk road at the small one-storey cottage opposite. An old man leaned on the garden gate, watching the busy scene in the field. On an impulse I crossed over and spoke to him: some casual remark about his roses. Soon I was able to lead the conversation round to the old house.

'Lot of people ask me about it,' he said. 'Whether it's for sale and that. But none of 'em ever come back, so I suppose there must be some kind of legal problem I don't know about.'

'Been empty long, has it?' I asked.

'Lord, yes. Years and years. Last chap as had it was a foreigner, Dutch or Belgian or some such. Surly beggar – I thought, anyways.' He recounted an involved and hard-to-follow tale of how his 'neighbourly call' had been rebuffed by the new occupant and then went into a recollection of the arrival of the foreigner's luggage. 'Crates and crates of stuff. As the carriers were unloading the cart he come to the door and cursed them for their slowness, and whether it was his nasty croakin' voice or what, I don't know, but the horses reared and nearly bolted, and a crate fell off the back of the cart and bust. Books all over the drive, there were.' He chuckled maliciously. 'He was in a rare takin', the Dutchman was. I really thought he would fly at the men.'

I took my leave of the old gossip at last and returned to my hotel. I'd brought my books down with me and after dinner I spent the evening studying. It seemed unlikely that the equipment would arrive for some days, and I was determined to put the time to good use.

Next day the weather had changed for the better, and my good intentions evaporated. It was far too pleasant a day to spend in my room. I went for a stroll round the little market town. There wasn't much to see, but one thing did catch my attention: a solicitor's office. I studied the brass name-plate on the wall for a time, then went up the narrow stairs to the office and enquired about the empty house.

I had struck lucky; they held the keys to it, though naturally the assistant was reluctant to hand them over to me until I produced evidence of the fact that I was from the firm connected with the development. After checking with someone in another office he gave them to me, and I returned in triumph to my midday meal.

After lunch I drove out of town and up the now-familiar road to the site. The big iron key turned the lock in the front door easily enough, though the rusting hinges groaned in protest as I pushed in.

Inside, I found the ground floor rooms still completely furnished and carpeted, with a thick layer of dust over everything. I detected the odour of dry rot, and kept to the wall side of the staircase as I climbed.

The first floor was in the same mouldering condition. From the window of one side bedroom I could see the site spread below, and was struck by the contrast between that busy scene and the stillness that enveloped the old house. It was as though I watched another world, a place far removed from me in space and time. I spotted MacFadyen on the other side of the field, a tiny figure beside a toy lorry. His minute arm pointed and waved. I turned away, brushing against the rotting fabric of the curtain beside me, and it fell in a cloud of dust. In the field below, a workman paused in his digging and stared curiously up at the window.

There was a small steep staircase leading to the top floor. I ascended them cautiously, testing each tread before putting my weight on it. At the top, I found myself in a small passageway with four doors leading off it. The first room contained only a rusty iron bedstead half-covered in plaster from the collapsing ceiling. The second held four or five wooden crates, all empty.

The third, a larger room, was crammed with books. They were stacked on shelves, laid on chairs, on the bare wooden floor and even on the narrow mantelpiece. I picked up volumes at random. Some of the titles were known to me: the infamous *Cultes des Goules* of Comte d'Erlette; Alhazred's *Necronomicon* – a comparatively modern translation, this, in Latin; Doctor Hugh Lamb's seventeenth-century *Dissertation on Witchcraft*, which under the guise of a scholarly treatise had disseminated unholy beliefs and practices until it was declared a banned book by the Church.

Others were unknown to me: books of which I had never heard, nor ever want to again. There was one called *De Vermis Mysteriis*, by a Ludwig Prinn; *Unaussprechlichen Kulten* by von Junzt, and *The Alchemy of Immortality*, by Abbot Martin – this last containing some of the most repugnant and frightening woodcuts it is possible to imagine. I snapped it shut and dropped it with a shudder. Its fall aroused distant echoes in some other part of the house.

Returning to the passage, I tried the fourth door, and here I found a curious thing: a huge brass padlock was fastened in a steel hasp firmly screwed to door and jamb. It had evidently been in position for some considerable time, for the brass was green with verdigris and the steel was coated in rust. Nevertheless, it still held the door firmly shut, as I found when I pushed at it with my shoulder. A faint rustle from within suggested the presence of rats, or possibly the ceiling had fallen in here as it had in the other room, and birds had got in. But why lock this room, and leave the priceless old books in the other room?

I returned thoughtfully down the two flights of stairs, somehow unable to shake off the feeling that I was being watched by some unseen observer. By the time I reached the hall I was actually hurrying to get out, and I found myself listening to the echoes of my steps, which seemed to come by some acoustic trick from just behind me.

Outside again in the weed-choked garden, I felt an almost physical oppression lift from me. The workman I had seen from the window leaned on his spade and pushed his cap to the back of his head. I knew that most of the labour force employed here were local men; perhaps I could glean some more information from him. I found a gap in the hedge and walked across.

He seemed to welcome the break in his work, and gave my question lengthy thought before replying.

'The Dutchman? Yes, I can remember him livin' there, all right. I was a nipper then, o' course, but I recall my mother and father tellin' me strict-like not to go playin' anywheres near this house. That was after he'd got the place a bad reppitation, with all sorts o' goings-on.'

'Why, what sort of goings-on?' I asked. 'Parties, you mean?'

'Well, not exactly. But car-loads of folk would arrive, sometimes, from London it was said, and not very pleasant-looking either, some of 'em. Then they stopped, just like that, and never came no more.

'And there was some talk of cockerels goin' missin' from one or two of the farms nearby, though how that could be laid at the Dutchman's door I can't rightly see. Even a missin' goat was blamed on him, once. Mind you, he only had himself to blame for not bein' popular, for 'e was a surly type. I can remember my Dad, he was postman in them days, God rest his soul, tellin' my mother about how the Dutchman would snatch a parcel out of his hand when he had cycled all the way up here with it, and heavy parcels they were too. Books, as my Dad reckoned.'

He paused to take breath, and I remarked, 'He seems to have left most of them when he left: I've just been in there, and there is a room full of them.'

'Aye, I seen you. That was a queer thing, the way he went away sudden-like. It wasn't till a man from the Town Hall called about something – the rates not bein' paid, something like that – that it was found that he was gone, and in the end the police were called in. Me and some of my mates were playin' in the woods there, that day, and saw Sergeant Hewitt come out to the house with two or three other men. They got in all right, then the next thing we saw was Father Cunningham from the RC chapel in the town going in, and things were brought out wrapped in sheets, and we saw smoke goin' up in the back garden. But what that was all about I don't know.'

At this point MacFadyen appeared, striding over the fields towards us, and the workman bent to his digging again with a muttered 'O' Lor''. However, I met the supervisor on my way back to the road, and was able to convince him that my enquiries and conversation had been of a technical nature and concerned drainage and subsoil, and I think I averted his wrath from the historian in the trench.

The next day – Thursday – I received a telegram from Turner saying that the replacement instruments would not arrive at the site until Saturday at the earliest. Instead of being dismayed at the prospect of an extended stay in Boarwood, my reaction was one of satisfaction; my first thought being that I could now investigate further the old house and its past. It was strange, though I did not think of it at the time, how the place had laid hold of my mind.

I found a copy of the local weekly paper in the hotel lounge, and made a note of the address of its offices. Fifteen minutes later I was leafing through back numbers of the paper at their reception desk. The key I had been given had had a label tied to it marked 'Bretton Manor, Fr. D.' and it was this name I sought as my eyes ran over the pages.

The first mention of the name was in a house-agent's advertisement: 'Bretton Manor. A Fine Detached Country Residence on the Boarwood–Reading road, with Fine Views over—' and so on. Among other things, the advert stated that the house was 'Part-Elizabethan', which confirmed my estimate of its age.

The next thing to catch my eye was a news item in an issue dated several years later; 1936 I think. It told of the discovery in the garden of Bretton Manor of the body of a tramp. He was identified as the same man who had been ejected from one or two pubs in the town on the evening of his death, and had evidently broken into the empty house. The report went on: 'The dead man, who was aged about fifty, was found lying in the bushes at the side of the house. It is thought that he had fallen from an upper window.'

I laid the paper aside, visualizing the scene in my mind. The nearest bushes at the side of the house were a good ten or twelve feet from it; a remarkable distance for a man of fifty to clear, I thought. The unfortunate man had, it appeared, died from severe lacerations to the face and neck, caused by the glass of the window through which he had fallen.

I returned the papers to the girl behind the desk, and made my way round to the solicitor's office to return the key. As I did so I asked the assistant if his firm held the deeds to the manor. He did not know, but summoned a senior clerk.

'The Bretton property? No, we do not have any documents relating to it. As we have informed your firm's legal representatives, they were originally in the hands of Russell and Brambell, and were lost when that firm's premises were burned down in 1939.'

I thanked him, received a frigid nod in reply, and returned to my hotel in time for lunch.

I made a determined attempt to study in my room in the afternoon, for my exams were not too far distant, but was unable to concentrate. Again and again I caught myself thinking of the ill-mannered Dutchman of Bretton Manor, or of the tramp who had died a lonely death there after the occupant's disappearance. In the end I threw my book aside and lay on the bed. The drone of traffic in the street below faded as I dozed.

I woke sweating from some half-remembered nightmare and sat up on the bed, letting the prosaic normality of the room sink into my mind. The dream was not wholly dispelled, however; I could recall most of it. It had begun innocently enough. I seemed to be one among a throng of party guests, sharing in their gaiety and laughter. But as time went on, I began to see that they were not all that they seemed. A pretty girl swept past me, smiling, and I saw that her golden hair was a clever wig, that her skin was unnatural-looking, and that her eyes were the eyes of an old, old woman.

A voice behind me said, 'Nicolas has prepared the room for the service. A black cockerel, this time.' I turned, but the speaker had not been addressing me. I made my way through the crowd, their false mirth ringing in my ears, and climbed many stairs. At last I found myself in a narrow passageway; a familiar passageway, I thought. This time the rooms were clean, and in the room which held the books a bright electric lamp burned. I passed it, and pushed open the door of the fourth room. It was not locked now.

As I entered the man in the centre of the room turned his head. He wore a long dirty coat and ragged trousers. His chin was bristly and unshaven. But why should his eyes widen in terror as he looked past me, and why did his mouth open in a soundless shriek? He backed away, his fist pressed to his mouth, then turned and leapt at the window behind him. I stared aghast as he vanished in a storm of breaking glass. Then I felt a hand rest on my shoulder . . .

It was at that point that I awoke. I sat for some minutes, trying to decide what the croaking voice in my ear had said as I jerked out of sleep. Then I went to the little basin at the hotel window and dashed cold water in my face. 'Really, you are letting the thought of that house obsess you,' I told my reflection in the mirror, 'and the best cure for that kind of silliness is a few drinks in a well-lighted bar.'

That evening, instead of going up to my room, I went into the little lounge bar next to the dining room. But it was too quiet, and the few other customers sat talking in twos and threes. I left after one drink, feeling aggrieved, and went down the road to a public bar.

This, too, was not as busy as I might have wished, but I did fall into conversation with two old chaps at the next table. They enquired, knowing I suppose from my accent that I was not a native of the town, what my business was. I explained briefly, and one of them nodded.

'Ah, that'll be the workings up on the Reading Road, opposite old Charlie's place.' And then, as if a malignant Fate had decreed that I should not spend an evening without being reminded of the old house, he went on: 'I expect they'll be pulling down the old Manor now.'

'Not before time, too,' chipped in his companion. 'Should've been done away with years ago, it should.'

'Why's that?' I asked. The drinks were beginning to take effect; not that I was slurring the words, but I had to exercise a conscious effort to enunciate them.

He laughed quickly, almost as though he was embarrassed at having revealed some belief which an outsider might not share.

'Oh, it had a bit of a bad name round here, before the war. Still has, really. That's all.'

'Didn't the last owner die suddenly or something?' I asked.

'Not exactly. But he did leave without telling anyone or taking any of his things. That caused a bit of a stir at the time, as you can imagine.'

'A furriner,' declared the other suddenly, 'And you never can tell with them.'

I agreed solemnly that foreigners were unpredictable creatures. The evening passed with astonishing quickness, and we parted on the pavement outside the pub with mutual good cheer.

I did not feel like going back to the hotel. I leaned against the car-park railings. A kind of fuddled resentment against Bretton Manor filled my mind, and I tried with drunken intentness to rationalize it. 'Frightened?' I asked myself. 'Why should I be frightened? Of course the locals have built up a thing about it over the years. Sup'stitious peasants, all of 'em.' Two girls hurried past, giggling, and I realized I had spoken the last words aloud. Picking my steps with exaggerated care, I went into the car-park with an air of injured dignity. 'No one goes near the place, especially at night, the old chap in the pub said.' I fumbled my keys from my pocket and opened the car door. 'Very well, I will go there tonight. That ought to prove . . .' I abandoned the muddled thought as I concentrated on driving the car out through the sleepy town and on to the Reading road.

Bretton Manor, picked out by the moonlight, was a black-and-white sketch silhouetted against the sky. I switched off the engine and let the car roll bumping on to the verge. It was then I realized that I had no way of getting in; I had given back the key. This setback only increased my determination, however, and I rummaged in the dashboard locker until I found a large torch.

I was half-way across the field, heading towards the wooden hut, when I heard the fox. That is how still and quiet the night was – I heard him before I saw him appear out of the wood. He hardly bothered to give me a glance before he loped away. At the back of the shed I found what I was after: a stout steel crowbar. Within minutes I had found the gap in the hedge and slipped through into the garden.

At the door, crowbar in hand, I paused. Returning sobriety cautioned me against the action I was about to take. It was foolish, and it was criminal. But I knew that if I backed down now, I would look back for the rest of my life and say: 'I turned yellow' and always I would know a private shame at my cowardice. With a sudden heave I forced open the door and stepped into the hall.

Now I could use my torch without fear of being seen. I switched it on and its beam picked out the bottom of the stairs, leaving the rest of the hall in an even deeper darkness than before. Something seemed to move swiftly out of the circle of light and retreat beyond it up the stairs. A rat, possibly, though the motion suggested a bat; a flapping, swirling movement. I decided that it must have been a trick of the light, and advanced.

The stillness was like a dead weight on me. I could hear the blood rushing in my ears as I found my way up the stair. At the foot of the second flight I paused. Was that a low chuckle I had heard? No, it could not have been, I reassured myself; the house must be empty, for the door was locked when you forced it. How could anyone be here? And the old boy in the pub had said that no one ever went near Bretton Manor at night, hadn't he? I took a deep breath and went on.

The huge padlock appeared in the beam of the torch, and I hefted the crowbar – a comfortingly heavy weight in my hand – and moved slowly down the narrow passage. The room containing the books was on my left, and I flashed the light in there. A gold-embossed title gleamed back at me: *Satanic Worship in the Middle Ages*. It looked comparatively modern. The dust on the floorboards still visible between the piles of books looked as though it had been disturbed by something dragging on it – not the sort of marks I would have thought my shoes would have made on my first visit.

At the padlocked door I hesitated again as my doubts renewed themselves. Somehow it seemed even more criminal to break open this door than it had been to force my way in downstairs. But I had come all this way; why not take the opportunity to see what lay within? Besides, I reasoned, I was not going to actually steal anything. In any case, when the demolition men at last came in, I would be back in London.

It took several minutes of sweating and swearing effort to prise the lock and hasp off. It fell to the floor with a clatter, and I pushed open the door and entered.

It was a large room, with queer angles to walls and ceiling. My steps echoed as though I was walking in an empty church, and indeed as I shone the torch round I thought at first that I had broken into some kind of private chapel, for there was an altar-like table on a low platform at one end, covered with a gold cloth, and on it lay an overturned Cross. Behind hung long curtains that still retained their rich purple. The moon shone palely through a window opposite the door but the other window, I saw, was roughly boarded over with wooden planks.

Something clattered and rolled as my foot touched it. I picked it up and examined it curiously. It was a solid silver bowl, of great age I judged, and beautifully engraved. Some dried brown residue lay in the bottom. I walked to the table and laid it down, and set the crucifix upon its heavy base. And then I saw that the Cross was all wrong: the base had been fixed to its top, so that as I stood it upright it was upside down.

Something pale reflected the torchlight back from the folds of the gold cloth. It was a book, almost hidden in the gloom. I picked that up too, and moved to the window to allow the moonlight to supplement the torch's rays. A sudden movement caught the edge of my vision, and I felt my heart bound inside my ribs.

I saw a pale-faced young man with a book in one hand and a torch and crowbar in the other. I was looking at my reflection in a tall, floor-mounted mirror.

I smiled sheepishly at my start of fear, and wondered vaguely what it was about the mirror that was different from the rest of the stuff in the house. It was very old, with an ornately carved wooden frame and legs, but I could not for the life of me tell what it was that marked it out from anything else in the place. I shrugged and turned the book so that the moonlight fell on it.

It was written in Latin, not printed but written in fading ink. On the flyleaf were the words: 'To Brother Nicolas, with the Hope that the Contents will be as Efficacious to him as they have been to me.' Only this dedication was in English.

I began to read the first pages, murmuring them aloud as I went along, for I had not used my tenuous grasp of the language since leaving school.

Again a dim movement caught my attention. I looked up. This time it was not my own reflection, because I had moved to one side of the old mirror. As I looked, it came again; a twitching at the curtains behind the table. They were drawn back, and a tall figure emerged. He wore a long robe with a cowl pulled over his head, hiding the face.

I was observing this apparition, of course, in the mirror. But when I spun round to face the dais – there was no one there! I looked again at the glass, doubting my sanity, and there was the man reflected, stepping off the platform. As I stared unbelievingly I realized with an odd detachment what it was that had bothered me about the mirror. Everything else in the house was covered in dust – it was as clean and polished as though it stood in a showroom.

The approaching figure was nearer, much nearer, advancing with outstretched arms. Though my eyes could be deceived, my ears could not, and I heard behind me the soft rustle of his robe and the faint shuffle of bare feet. I whirled, and threw the heavy crowbar at the spot corresponding to that in the mirror. The metal bar stopped dead in mid-air about six feet away, and fell to the ground.

My eyes flew to the door. But to reach it I would have to dart within inches of that dread figure, and I knew instinctively that if I was seized by those thin hands, not only would I die, but I would be condemned to eternal damnation. I do not know how I knew this; it was a certainty in my mind, as one knows that fire burns.

I darted a last glance at the mirror beside me, saw the being was almost within reach of me, and turned and ran straight at the window. It was my only means of escape, the one the tramp had taken. It had killed him, and it would kill me, but death was preferable to the touch of the spectre behind me. As I went headlong through the glass I threw my hand up to cover my face, and felt a cold stinging pain on the back of it as the glass sliced in. From behind me I heard a croak of fury, then I was falling into darkness.

The bushes had grown and thickened since the night the tramp had died: I landed on a pliant, springy cushion of branches that broke my fall like a net. I was winded, but I was able to scramble up and plunge through the undergrowth like a hunted animal, and stagger out on to the silvery moonlit road.

I never saw the lorry, only heard a shriek of rubber and felt a numbing blow on the arm that spun me to the verge. The driver came running back, swearing with fright, and jerked me to my feet.

His shocked, 'Gawd, mate, your hand . . .' made me look down, and I saw without understanding the gaping wound and the yellow-ish gristle of the half-severed tendons, and the dark blood that pumped out of it. I don't remember anything after that.

I suppose I must have been in hospital quite a long time, though I don't seem to have any coherent memories of it, only the memory of sitting up in bed one night and shouting at a curtain that was blowing in a draught.

And there were doctors, of course: some to attend to my hand and some to attend to my mind. The hand healed quickly, leaving only the scar. My mind took a lot longer to heal.

When I finally left, they told me it might be a good idea to write down all my hallucination, and I have in fact found it very beneficial to have done it. Of course, they didn't call my story a hallucination, but I could tell that was what they were going to put in my file.

Young Collins called to see me when I'd been home a day or two. The legal problems were sorted out, he said; Bretton Manor had been pulled down. They found a lot of queer old books and stuff in there, he said; and best of all, a real secret passage. I fear his news did not interest me as much as he had expected, even when he told me about the skeleton they found there. The skeleton, he says, wore a long robe.

The doctors were right; I do feel better for having written it all down. Perhaps now the dreams will stop.

# Stephen King
# The boogeyman

'I came to you because I want to tell my story,' the man on Dr Harper's couch was saying. The man was Lester Billings from Waterbury, Connecticut. According to the history taken from Nurse Vickers, he was twenty-eight, employed by an industrial firm in New York, divorced, and the father of three children. All deceased.

'I can't go to a priest because I'm not Catholic. I can't go to a lawyer because I haven't done anything to consult a lawyer about. All I did was kill my kids. One at a time. Killed them all.'

Dr Harper turned on the tape recorder.

Billings lay straight as a yardstick on the couch, not giving it an inch of himself. His feet protruded stiffly over the end. Picture of a man enduring necessary humiliation. His hands were folded corpselike on his chest. His face was carefully set. He looked at the plain white composition ceiling as if seeing scenes and pictures played out there.

'Do you mean you actually killed them, or—'

'No.' Impatient flick of the hand. 'But I was responsible. Denny in 1967. Shirl in 1971. And Andy this year. I want to tell you about it.'

Dr Harper said nothing. He thought that Billings looked haggard and old. His hair was thinning, his complexion sallow. His eyes held all the miserable secrets of whiskey.

'They were murdered, see? Only no one believes that. If they would, things would be all right.'

'Why is that?'

'Because . . .'

Billings broke off and darted up on his elbows, staring across the room. 'What's that?' he barked. His eyes had narrowed to black slots.

'What's what?'

'That door.'

'The closet,' Dr Harper said. 'Where I hang my coat and leave my overshoes.'

'Open it. I want to see.'

Dr Harper got up wordlessly, crossed the room, and opened the closet. Inside, a tan raincoat hung on one of four or five hangers. Beneath that was a pair of shiny galoshes. The New York *Times* had been carefully tucked into one of them. That was all.

'All right?' Dr Harper said.

'All right,' Billings removed the props of his elbows and returned to his previous position.

'You were saying,' Dr Harper said as he went back to his chair, 'that if the murder of your three children could be proved, all your troubles would be over. Why is that?'

'I'd go to gaol,' Billings said immediately. 'For life. And you can see into all the rooms in a gaol. All the rooms.' He smiled at nothing.

'How were your children murdered?'

'Don't try to jerk it out of me!'

Billings twitched around and stared balefully at Harper.

'I'll tell you, don't worry. I'm not one of your freaks, strutting around and pretending to be Napoleon or explaining that I got hooked on heroin because my mother didn't love me. I know you won't believe me. I don't care. It doesn't matter. Just to tell will be enough.'

'All right.' Dr Harper got out his pipe.

'I married Rita in 1965 – I was twenty-one and she was eighteen. She was pregnant. That was Denny.' His lips twisted in a rubbery, frightening grin that was gone in a wink. 'I had to leave college and get a job, but I didn't mind. I loved both of them. We were very happy.

'Rita got pregnant just a little while after Denny was born, and Shirl came along in December of 1966. Andy came in the summer of 1969, and Denny was already dead by then. Andy was an accident. That's what Rita said. She said sometimes that birth-control stuff doesn't work. I think that it was more than an accident. Children tie a man down, you know. Women like that, especially when the man is brighter than they. Don't you find that's true?'

108

Harper grunted noncommittally.

'It doesn't matter, though. I loved him anyway.' He said it almost vengefully, as if he had loved the child to spite his wife.

'Who killed the children?' Harper asked.

'The boogeyman,' Lester Billings answered immediately. 'The boogeyman killed them all. Just came out of the closet and killed them.' He twisted around and grinned. 'You think I'm crazy, all right. It's written all over you. But I don't care. All I want to do is tell you and then get lost.'

'I'm listening,' Harper said.

'It started when Denny was almost two and Shirl was just an infant. He started crying when Rita put him to bed. We had a two-bedroomed place, see. Shirl slept in a crib in our room. At first I thought he was crying because he didn't have a bottle to take to bed anymore. Rita said don't make an issue of it, let it go, let him have it and he'll drop it on his own. But that's the way kids start off bad. You get permissive with them, spoil them. Then they break your heart. Get some girl knocked up, you know, or start shooting dope. Or they get to be sissies. Can you imagine waking up some morning and finding your kid – your *son* – is a sissy?

'After a while, though, when he didn't stop, I started putting him to bed myself. And if he didn't stop crying I'd give him a whack. Then Rita said he was saying "light" over and over again. Well, I didn't know. Kids that little, how can you tell what they're saying. Only a mother can tell.

'Rita wanted to put in a nightlight. One of those wall-plug things with Mickey Mouse or Huckleberry Hound or something on it. I wouldn't let her. If a kid doesn't get over being afraid of the dark when he's little, he never gets over it.

'Anyway, he died the summer after Shirl was born. I put him to bed that night and he started to cry right off. I heard what he said that time. He pointed right at the closet when he said it. "Boogeyman," the kid says. "Boogeyman, Daddy."

'I turned off the light and went into our room and asked Rita why she wanted to teach the kid a word like that. I was tempted to slap her around a little, but I didn't. She said she never taught him to say that. I called her a goddamn liar.

'That was a bad summer for me, see. The only job I could get was

109

loading Pepsi-Cola trucks in a warehouse, and I was tired all the time. Shirl would wake up and cry every night and Rita would pick her up and sniffle. I tell you, sometimes I felt like throwing them both out a window. Christ, kids drive you crazy sometimes. You could kill them.

'Well, the kid woke me at three in the morning, right on schedule. I went to the bathroom, only a quarter awake, you know, and Rita asked me if I'd check on Denny. I told her to do it herself and went back to bed. I was almost asleep when she started to scream.

'I got up and went in. The kid was dead on his back. Just as white as flour except for where the blood had . . . had sunk. Back of the legs, the head, the a— the buttocks. His eyes were open. That was the worst, you know. Wide open and glassy, like the eyes you see on a moosehead some guy put over his mantel. Like pictures you see of those gook kids over in Nam. But an American kid shouldn't look like that. Dead on his back. Wearing diapers and rubber pants because he'd been wetting himself again the last couple of weeks. Awful, I loved that kid.'

Billings shook his head slowly, then offered the rubbery, frightening grin again. 'Rita was screaming her head off. She tried to pick Denny up and rock him, but I wouldn't let her. The cops don't like you to touch any of the evidence. I know that—'

'Did you know it was the boogeyman then?' Harper asked quietly.

'Oh, no. Not then. But I did see one thing. It didn't mean anything to me then, but my mind stored it away.'

'What was that?'

'The closet door was open. Not much. Just a crack. But I knew I left it shut, see. There's dry-cleaning bags in there. A kid messes around with one of those and bango. Asphyxiation. You know that?'

'Yes. What happened then?'

Billings shrugged. 'We planted him.' He looked morbidly at his hands, which had thrown dirt on three tiny coffins.

'Was there an inquest?'

'Sure.' Billings' eyes flashed with sardonic brilliance. 'Some back-country fuckhead with a stethoscope and a black bag full of Junior Mints and a sheepskin from some cow college. Crib death, he

110

called it! You ever hear such a pile of yellow manure? The kid was three years old!'

'Crib death is most common during the first year,' Harper said carefully, 'but that diagnosis has gone on death certificates for children up to the age of five for want of a better—'

'*Bullshit!*' Billings spat out violently.

Harper relit his pipe.

'We moved Shirl into Denny's old room a month after the funeral. Rita fought it tooth and nail, but I had the last word. It hurt me, of course it did. Jesus, I loved having the kid in with us. But you can't get overprotective. You make a kid a cripple that way. When I was a kid my mom used to take me to the beach and then scream herself hoarse. "Don't go out so far! Don't go there! It's got an undertow! You only ate an hour ago! Don't go over your head!" Even to watch out for sharks, before God. So what happens? I can't even go near the water now. It's the truth. I get the cramps if I go near a beach. Rita got me to take her and the kids to Savin Rock once when Denny was alive. I got sick as a dog. I know, see? You can't overprotect kids. And you can't coddle yourself either. Life goes on. Shirl went right into Denny's crib. We sent the old mattress to the dump, though. I didn't want my girl to get any germs.

'So a year goes by. And one night when I'm putting Shirl into her crib she starts to yowl and scream and cry. "Boogeyman, Daddy, boogeyman, boogeyman!"

'That threw a jump into me. It was just like Denny. And I started to remember about that closet door, open just a crack when we found him. I wanted to take her into our room for the night.'

'Did you?'

'No.' Billings regarded his hands and his face twitched. 'How could I go to Rita and admit I was wrong? I *had* to be strong. She was always such a jellyfish . . . look how easy she went to bed with me when we weren't married.'

Harper said, 'On the other hand, look how easily *you* went to bed with *her*.'

Billings froze in the act of rearranging his hands and slowly turned his head to look at Harper. 'Are you trying to be a wise guy?'

'No, indeed,' Harper said.

'Then let me tell it my way,' Billings snapped. 'I came here to get this off my chest. To tell my story. I'm not going to talk about my sex life, if that's what you expect. Rita and I had a very normal sex life, with none of that dirty stuff. I know it gives some people a charge to talk about that, but I'm not one of them.'

'Okay,' Harper said.

'Okay,' Billings echoed with uneasy arrogance. He seemed to have lost the thread of his thought, and his eyes wandered uneasily to the closet door, which was firmly shut.

'Would you like that open?' Harper asked.

'No!' Billings said quickly. He gave a nervous little laugh. 'What do I want to look at your overshoes for?

'The boogeyman got her, too,' Billings said. He brushed at his forehead, as if sketching memories. 'A month later. But something happened before that. I heard a noise in there one night. And then she screamed. I opened at the door real quick – the hall light was on – and . . . she was sitting up in the crib crying and . . . something *moved*. Back in the shadows, by the closet. Something *slithered*.'

'Was the closet door open?'

'A little. Just a crack.' Billings licked his lips. 'Shirl was screaming about the boogeyman. And something else that sounded like "claws". Only she said "craws", you know. Little kids have trouble with that "l" sound. Rita ran upstairs and asked what the matter was. I said she got scared by the shadows of the branches moving on the ceiling.'

'Crawset?' Harper said.

'Huh?'

'Crawset . . . closet. Maybe she was trying to say "closet".'

'Maybe,' Billings said. 'Maybe that was it. But I don't think so. I think it was "claws".' His eyes began seeking the closet door again. 'Claws, long claws.' His voice had sunk to a whisper.

'Did you look in the closet?'

'Y-yes.' Billings' hands were laced tightly across his chest, laced tightly enough to show a white moon at each knuckle.

'Was there anything in there? Did you see the—'

'*I didn't see anything!*' Billings screamed suddenly. And the words poured out, as if a black cork had been pulled from the bottom of his soul: 'When she died I found her, see. And she was black. All black. She swallowed her own tongue and she was just as black as a nigger

112

in a minstrel show and she was staring at me. Her eyes, they looked like those eyes you see on stuffed animals, all shiny and awful, like live marbles, and they were saying it got me, Daddy, you let it get me, you killed me, you helped it kill me . . .' His words trailed off. One single tear very large and silent ran down the side of his cheek.

'It was a brain convulsion, see? Kids get those sometimes. A bad signal from the brain. They had an autopsy at Hartford Receiving and they told us she choked on her tongue from the convulsion. And I had to go home alone because they kept Rita under sedation. She was out of her mind. I had to go back to that house all alone, and I know a kid don't just get convulsions because their brain frigged up. You can scare a kid into convulsions. And I had to go back to the house where *it* was.'

He whispered, 'I slept on the couch. With the light on.'

'Did anything happen?'

'I had a dream,' Billings said. 'I was in a dark room and there was something I couldn't . . .couldn't quite see, in the closet. It made a noise . . . a squishy noise. It reminded me of a comic book I read when I was a kid. *Tales from the Crypt*, you remember that? Christ! They had a guy named Graham Ingles; he could draw every god-awful thing in the world – and some out of it. Anyway, in this story this woman drowned her husband, see? Put cement blocks on his feet and dropped him into a quarry. Only he came back. He was all rotted and black-green and the fish had eaten away one of his eyes and there was seaweed in his hair. He came back and killed her. And when I woke up in the middle of the night, I thought that would be leaning over me. With claws . . . long claws . . .'

Dr Harper looked at the digital clock inset into his desk. Lester Billings had been speaking for nearly half an hour. He said, 'When your wife came back home, what was her attitude towards you?'

'She still loved me,' Billings said with pride. 'She still wanted to do what I told her. That's the wife's place, right? This women's lib only makes sick people. The most important thing in life is for a person to know his place. His . . . his . . . uh . . .'

'Station in life?'

'That's it!' Billings snapped his fingers. 'That's it exactly. And a wife should follow her husband. Oh, she was sort of colourless the first four or five months after – dragged around the house, didn't sing, didn't watch the TV, didn't laugh. I knew she'd get over it. When they're that little, you don't get so attached to them. After a while you have to go to the bureau drawer and look at a picture to even remember exactly what they looked like.

'She wanted another baby,' he added darkly. 'I told her it was a bad idea. Oh, not for ever, but for a while. I told her it was a time for us to get over things and begin to enjoy each other. We never had a chance to do that before. If you wanted to go to a movie, you had to hassle around for a baby-sitter. You couldn't go into town to see the Mets unless her folks would take the kids, because my mom wouldn't have anything to do with us. Denny was born too soon after we were married, see? She said Rita was just a tramp, a common little corner-walker. Corner-walker is what my mom always called them. Isn't that a sketch? She sat me down once and told me diseases you can get if you went to a cor— to a prostitute. How your pri—, your penis has just a little tiny sore on it one day and the next day it's rotting right off. She wouldn't even come to the wedding.'

Billings drummed his chest with his fingers.

'Rita's gynaecologist sold her on this thing called an IUD – interuterine device. Foolproof, the doctor said. He just sticks it up the woman's . . . her place, and that's it. If there's anything in there, the egg can't fertilize. You don't even know it's there.' He smiled at the ceiling with dark sweetness. 'No one knows if it's there or not. And next year she's pregnant again. Some foolproof.'

'No birth-control method is perfect,' Harper said. 'The pill is only ninety-eight per cent. The IUD may be ejected by cramps, strong, menstrual flow, and, in exceptional cases, by evacuation.'

'Yeah. Or you can take it out.'

'That's possible.'

'So what's next? She's knitting little things, singing in the shower, and eating pickles like crazy. Sitting on my lap and saying things about how it must have been God's will. *Piss*.'

'The baby came at the end of the year after Shirl's death?'

'That's right. A boy. She named it Andrew Lester Billings. I didn't want anything to do with it, at least at first. My motto was she screwed up, so let her take care of it. I know how that sounds but you have to remember that I'd been through a lot.

'But I warmed up to him, you know it? He was the only one of the litter that looked like me, for one thing. Denny looked like his mother, and Shirl didn't look like anybody, except maybe my Grammy Ann. But Andy was the spitting image of me.

'I'd get to playing around with him in his playpen when I got home from work. He'd grab only my finger and smile and gurgle. Nine weeks old and the kid was grinning up at his old dad. You believe that?

'Then one night, here I am coming out of a drugstore with a mobile to hang over the kid's crib. Me! Kids don't appreciate presents until they're old enough to say thank you, that was always my motto. But there I was, buying him silly crap and all at once I realize I love him the most of all. I had another job by then, a pretty good one, selling drill bits for Cluett and Sons. I did real well, and when Andy was one, we moved to Waterbury. The old place had too many bad memories.

'And too many closets.

'That next year was the best one for us. I'd give every finger on my right hand to have it back again. Oh, the war in Vietnam was still going on, and the hippies were still running around with no clothes on, and the niggers were yelling a lot, but none of that touched us. We were on a quiet street with nice neighbours. We were happy,' he summed up simply. 'I asked Rita once if she wasn't worried. You know bad luck comes in threes and all that. She said not for us. She said Andy was special. She said God had drawn a ring around him.'

Billings looked morbidly at the ceiling.

'Last year wasn't so good. Something about the house changed. I started keeping my boots in the hall because I didn't like to open the closet door anymore. I kept thinking: Well, what if it's in there? All crouched down and ready to spring the second I open the door? And I'd started thinking I could hear squishy noises, as if something black and green and wet was moving around in there just a little.

'Rita asked me if I was working too hard, and I started to snap at her, just like the old days. I got sick to my stomach leaving them alone to go to work, but I was glad to get out. God help me, I was glad to get out. I started to think, see, that it lost us for a while when we moved. It had to hunt around, slinking through the streets at night and maybe creeping in the sewers. Smelling for us. It took a year, but it found us. It's back. It wants Andy and it wants me. I started to think, maybe if you think of a thing long enough, and believe in it, it gets real. Maybe all the monsters we were scared of when we were kids, Frankenstein and Wolfman and Mummy, maybe they were real. Real enough to kill the kids that were supposed to have fallen into gravel pits or drowned in lakes or were just never found. Maybe . . .'

'Are you backing away from something, Mr Billings?'

Billings was silent for a long time – two minutes clicked off the digital clock. Then he said abruptly: 'Andy died in February. Rita wasn't there. She got a call from her father. Her mother had been in a car crash the day after New Year's and wasn't expected to live. She took a bus back that night.

'Her mother didn't die, but she was on the critical list for a long time – two months. I had a very good woman who stayed with Andy days. We kept house nights. And closet doors kept coming open.'

Billings licked his lips. 'The kid was sleeping in the room with me. It's funny, too. Rita asked me once when he was two if I wanted to move him into another room. Spock or one of those other quacks claims its bad for kids to sleep with their parents, see? Supposed to give them traumas about sex and all that. But we never did it unless the kid was asleep. And I didn't want to move him. I was afraid to, after Denny and Shirl.'

'But you did move him, didn't you?' Dr Harper asked.

'Yeah,' Billings said. He smiled a sick, yellow smile. 'I did.'

Silence again. Billings wrestled with it.

'I had to!' he barked finally. 'I had to! It was all right when Rita was there, but when she was gone, it started to get bolder. It started . . .' He rolled his eyes at Harper and bared his teeth in a savage grin. 'Oh, you won't believe it. I know what you think, just another goofy for your casebook, I know that, but you weren't there, you lousy smug head-peeper.

'One night every door in the house blew wide open. One morning I got up and found a trail of mud and filth across the hall between the coat closet and the front door. Was it going out? Coming in? I don't know! Before Jesus, I just don't know! Records all scratched up and covered with slime, mirrors broken . . . and the sounds . . . the sounds . . .'

He ran a hand through his hair. 'You'd wake up at three in the morning and look into the dark and at first you'd say, "It's only the clock." But underneath it you could hear something moving in a stealthy way. But not too stealthy, because it wanted you to hear it. A slimy sliding sound like something from the kitchen drain. Or a clicking sound, like claws being dragged lightly over the staircase banister. And you'd close your eyes, knowing that hearing it was bad, but if you *saw* it . . .

'And always you'd be afraid that the noises might stop for a little while, and then there would be a laugh right over your face and a breath of air like stale cabbage on your face, and then hands on your throat.'

Billings was pallid and trembling.

'So I moved him. I knew it would go for him, see. Because he was weaker. And it did. That very first night he screamed in the middle of the night and finally, when I got up the cojones to go in, he was standing up in bed and screaming, "The boogeyman, Daddy . . . boogeyman . . . wanna go wif Daddy, go wif Daddy." ' Billings' voice had become a high treble, like a child's. His eyes seemed to fill his entire face; he almost seemed to shrink on the couch.

'But I couldn't,' the childish breaking treble continued, 'I couldn't. And an hour later there was a scream. An awful, gurgling scream. And I knew how much I loved him because I ran in, I didn't even turn on the light, I ran, ran, *ran*, oh, Jesus God Mary, it had him; it was shaking him, shaking him just like a terrier shakes a piece of cloth and I could see something with awful slumped shoulders and a scarecrow head and I could smell something like a dead mouse in a pop bottle and I heard . . .' He trailed off, and then his voice clicked back into an adult range. 'I heard it when Andy's neck broke.' Billings' voice was cool and dead. 'It made a sound like ice cracking when you're skating on a country pond in winter.'

'Then what happened?'

'Oh, I ran,' Billings said in the same cool, dead voice. 'I went to an all-night diner. How's that for complete cowardice? Ran to an all-night diner and drank six cups of coffee. Then I went home. It was already dawn. I called the police even before I went upstairs.

He was lying on the floor and staring at me. Accusing me. A tiny bit of blood had run out of one ear. Only a drop, really. And the closet door was open – but just a crack.'

The voice stopped. Harper looked at the digital clock. Fifty minutes had passed.

'Make an appointment with the nurse,' he said. 'In fact, several of them. Tuesdays and Thursdays?'

'I only came to tell my story,' Billings said. 'To get it off my chest. I lied to the police, see? Told them the kid must have tried to get out of his crib in the night and . . . they swallowed it. Course they did. That's just what it looked like. Accidental, like the others. But Rita knew. Rita . . . finally . . . knew . . .'

He covered his eyes with his right arm and began to weep.

'Mr Billings, there is a great deal to talk about,' Dr Harper said after a pause. 'I believe we can remove some of the guilt you've been carrying, but first you have to want to get rid of it.'

'Don't you believe I *do?*' Billings cried, removing his arm from his eyes. They were red, raw, wounded.

'Not yet,' Harper said quietly. 'Tuesdays and Thursdays?'

After a long silence, Billings muttered, 'Goddamn shrink. All right. All right.'

'Make an appointment with the nurse, Mr Billings. And have a good day.'

Billings laughed emptily and walked out of the office quickly, without looking back.

The nurse's station was empty. A small sign on the desk blotter said: 'Back in a Minute.'

Billings turned and went back into the office. 'Doctor, your nurse is—'

The room was empty.

But the closet door was open. Just a crack.

'So nice,' the voice from the closet said. 'So nice.' The words sounded as if they might have come through a mouthful of rotted seaweed.

Billings stood rooted to the spot as the closet door swung open. He dimly felt warmth at his crotch as he wet himself.

'So nice,' the boogeyman said as it shambled out.

It still held its Dr Harper mask in one rotted, spade-claw hand.

# Alan Ryan
# Tell mommy what happened

His parents knew Robbie was strange. And just a little scary. Robbie . . . saw . . . things.

At three, he had not yet mastered enough language to express or describe with any clarity the odd things he saw, the distant images or scraps of ideas that entered his mind unbidden, unsought, like leaves drifting on a breeze. Nor did he have the age or insight to recognize the images or ideas as strange. Children's minds are not like ours. And Robbie's mind was not like other children's. Not at all.

He was the loveliest child to look at. Light brown hair curled like wisps of fragile silk around his head. His porcelain ears were so perfectly formed – the whorls like those of the rarest seashell – that their intricacy was almost a proof for the existence of God. His skin glowed pink with an inner light that seemed to mould the baby flesh with health. A lovely child to look at.

Margaret Lockwood adored her son. She loved him all the more for having lost two children in miscarriages before him. She had invested four months flat on her back in bed to give Robbie life. Oh, she loved him.

David Lockwood, as often as he smiled at the beauty and perfection of his tiny son, even more often stared in wonder at him: How could such a beautiful thing exist? How could they have made such a thing? How? And in the stillness of the night-time house, his hand would grope in the nursery's half light for the hand of his wife and squeeze, squeeze. Imagine! Just look at him!

But there were other times, too, when Margaret and David Lockwood stared at Robbie. In silence. With a different kind of wonder.

Robbie saw things. Things other people did not see. Things he could know nothing about. It was very strange how Robbie could see things.

As far as Margaret and David Lockwood could determine, Robbie began to see things about the time he first began to talk. It was, of course, possible that he had been seeing things before that. There was no way to tell for sure; he may have been simply unable to articulate the things he saw. They preferred – without actually discussing the matter at any great length – not to examine the question too closely. It made them uneasy. And Robbie was too perfect a child to think of in odd terms.

But when he began to talk, the odd things were there.

As Margaret Lockwood was putting Robbie to bed one evening, he suddenly squirmed in her arms. She almost dropped him and had to set him quickly on his feet before he fell. As soon as he was on the floor, Robbie looked up into her face and smiled happily.

'Daddy,' he said. 'Flashlight.'

Margaret Lockwood crouched in front of her lovely son and put her hands gently on his shoulders to hold him in place.

'What, Robbie?' she said.

'Daddy,' Robbie said again, his smile widening, lighting up his face. 'Daddy have flashlight.'

Then he turned and scampered off to his room.

His mother rose and followed him into the nursery. While she was getting him ready for bed, she said again – gently, lightly, coaxingly, 'Does Daddy have a flashlight?' She kept smiling.

Robbie ignored her and amused himself by trying to pull the sheet loose from the mattress.

'Robbie, does Daddy have a flashlight?'

But Robbie's mind was far away, his ears deaf to her question. Margaret Lockwood was certain that Robbie knew nothing of any flashlight Daddy might have at the moment. She was uncertain if Robbie had ever used the word 'flashlight' before. She thought not.

David Lockwood was a fireman and that week he was working the night shift. When he worked nights, it was his habit to call Margaret from the firehouse around midnight – timing it carefully not to interrupt her 11:00 news or Johnny Carson's monologue – to let her know that everything was all right, and to say good night. They missed each other when he had to work nights.

When David called that night, Margaret was dozing on the couch while the television chuckled at her. The phone startled her awake. She had it to her ear before she realized it was David making his nightly call.

'Quiet tonight,' David said. 'We only had one alarm all evening. Some old lady's frozen pizza went up in smoke in her oven. Only took us about ten minutes.'

'Oh, good, David,' Margaret said. She was yawning.

'What took time was getting back to the house. The damn truck broke down and yours truly ended up squiggling around underneath it for half an hour. And that truck's not exactly built like the Volks. But I got it—'

'Your truck broke down?'

'Yeah. But relax, honey, it was no big deal. We lost a hose, that's all. The only problem I had was getting at the damn thing. Took me—'

'Where were you when it happened?'

'Where? Oh, somewhere on Route 18. We were on our way back.'

Margaret had stopped yawning. 'Was it dark?'

David laughed. 'Nah, the sun came out and shone right on the bottom of the truck. Honey, of course it was dark. And just for good measure, two of the flashlights went dead.'

'But you had one? I mean, *you* had one?'

'Yes, I had one. Margaret? Is something wrong? You sound strange.'

When David returned home a little after 4:30, he found Margaret asleep on the couch instead of in bed. The television was still on, the voices turned down to a distant blur of human sound, just enough to keep her company in the night.

It was just an odd coincidence, they decided in the morning.

But it was not. In the next few months they realized that Robbie really did *see* things. Odd things.

A few months after this third birthday, Robbie began talking to an imaginary playmate called Alec. He would sit out on the lawn or the front steps or in the back yard and mumble away happily to himself for hours on end, apparently chatting with the invisible Alec. When Margaret's girl friends and neighbours came in for coffee, they commented, smiling, and Margaret would laugh with them. Oh, she would say, Alec was a godsend, she didn't know what she would do without him. He kept Robbie busy for hours at a time without a grumble. Better than television for keeping him occupied and out of her hair. He was the best baby-sitter in the world. And the price was right. And he didn't have to be driven home afterwards.

Occasionally she would notice on Robbie's face a look of rapt attention as he appeared to be listening to Alec. She assumed it was Alec. There were moments when it bothered her a bit. But her girl friends' children had imaginary playmates too. Some of them did. A few of them.

But it really didn't bother Margaret Lockwood a great deal. At least it didn't bother her anymore than Robbie's *seeing* things. In fact, the only thing that bothered her at all was the fact that Alec, it seemed, never came into the house. And the only reason that fact got even that much of her attention was that she could have used his help sometimes in the evening to keep Robbie company. The boy was now at an age where he was constantly on the move, exploring, poking into everything, his curiosity and his imagination both working overtime. By evening, Margaret was often exhausted. She wanted Robbie in bed and the evening to herself, especially when David was working nights. In fact, with Robbie at this active stage, she welcomed the evenings alone. After dinner, she would kiss David goodbye and put Robbie to bed and actually look forward to spending the evening alone, relaxing with a magazine or dozing in front of the television. On those evenings, she seemed to sleep so much better on the couch than she ever did in bed. And she still got a normal night's sleep.

But Robbie, refreshed from an afternoon nap, was often a bundle of energy in the evenings. Or, even without the nap, he was too excited, too overactive, too overtired, too *something*, to fall asleep immediately.

On those evenings, Margaret wished Alec would come inside. She would try to coax Robbie into imagining the invisible friend right there in the nursery, right there beside him. But Robbie wouldn't have it. She had no luck. Alec, it seemed, would not set foot – if that was the right word for it – inside the house. No Alec. And little rest for Margaret Lockwood that night.

On those evenings, she wished fervently that Robbie would *see* Alec inside the house.

But he would not.


One day Robbie was standing in the middle of the back yard and his mother thought there was something odd about the way he was standing and . . . looking? She couldn't be sure. She started outside, then grabbed quickly at the screen door to keep it from slamming behind her. Robbie's back was turned. He was staring at the fence at the back of the yard and had no idea his mother was watching him. It was the angle of his head that had caught her eye. It was cocked curiously to one side with the unabashed honesty of children. He just stood, feet apart at an awkward angle, as if he had been running and had been forced to a sudden halt. By what? His body was still, frozen, head tilted to one side. Margaret Lockwood watched her son. She knew that Robbie was *seeing* something. Suddenly Robbie whirled and ran back toward the house. His eyes were wide. They flew open wider as he spotted her in the doorway. His little legs pumped hard across the manicured grass of the yard, up the brick steps, into the waiting arms of his mother.

'Did something frighten you, Robbie?' she said, her voice already crooning, comforting, accustomed to banishing the fears of childhood.

Robbie stood stiffly in her arms, his body leaning back and away from her slightly.

'Alec . . .' he said. And stopped.

She touched the back of his head, the back of his neck.

'What about Alec, honey?'

Robbie's eyes widened in childish astonishment.

'He walked through the wall.'

Margaret Lockwood looked into her son's face.

'He walked through the wall,' Robbie said again. His voice expressed amazement as only a child's can: amazement unparalleled and beyond a child's powers to feign.

'He walked through the wall?' his mother said, her voice flitting between disbelief, encouragement, and fright.

Robbie's head bobbed up and down. 'Yup,' he said, 'right through the wall.'

Three weeks after Robbie saw Alec walk through the wall, the boy came running inside to his mother shortly after she had sent him out to the yard to play. She was sitting at the kitchen table, having another cup of coffee and listening to the radio as Robbie came crashing into the house. She spilled coffee all over the table and had to grab at the boy to keep him from being splashed and burned.

'Mommy! Mommy!'

He had to catch his breath before he could tell her why he was so excited.

'Robbie, what is it?'

His eyes were gleaming. 'Alec . . .' he said.

He stood there, panting heavily.

'Robbie!'

He took a step backward, away from his mother.

'Robbie, what's wrong? Robbie!'

The boy was solemn-faced now, his eyes openly gazing at her. With curiosity? If Robbie had been older, his mother would have described the look on his face as 'speculative', as if he were weighing possibilities, making some sort of judgment. But Robbie was only three, too young for anything like that. Much too young.

'Nothing,' he said. And he was gone, the kitchen door left to slam loudly behind him.

Margaret Lockwood jumped from the table to follow her son. As she moved, she spilled the remaining coffee from her cup. She swore, hesitated, stopped to wipe it up quickly. By the time she got to the back yard in search of Robbie, the boy was playing with one of his trucks. It was a big red fire engine, made of heavy-gauge steel and weighing, Margaret Lockwood often thought when she had to move it, almost as much as Robbie himself. Its value, David had explained when he brought it home, was in the authenticity of the details. It was fitted with a little seat on top and could be wheeled, slowly, by a boy of Robbie's age and strength. Robbie was sitting on it now, leaning forward, fingers gripping the cab of the truck, knees and legs straining to push it through the grass of the yard. The boy didn't see her; the truck and its weight absorbed all his attention.

Margaret Lockwood stood in the doorway for a moment, watching him, then let the door close silently. Through the screen she continued to watch her son. After a while she decided not to go outside. Robbie was lost in his play with the truck. He would push it a foot or so – two good shoves with his sturdy legs – then stop to rest. Each time he stopped, he would look back over his shoulder, as if he were looking up into somebody's face, almost as if he were seeking approval for how he had moved the heavy truck. Each time he did it, Margaret Lockwood could see his lips move, but she couldn't hear what he was saying. Of course it didn't matter. Robbie was talking to Alec.

That evening she spoke to her husband about Robbie. She told him about the episode that morning. She told him about some of the other strange things that had happened in recent months, as many as she could remember, ones that she had not mentioned to him at the time they occurred. She told him some things that might not have been episodes at all, just little things that, for some reason, had made her uneasy for a moment. She told him everything she could think of about Robbie that had struck her, even for an instant, as strange. She told him about Alec, about Alec walking through the wall, and how she believed it, believed it because Robbie himself had been genuinely puzzled, about how Robbie talked to Alec when he rode the fire truck, about how Alec would not come into the house, no matter how much she coaxed. She told David everything.

He did not exactly make light of it but he saw no cause for concern either. Children had incredible imaginations, he said, remember that. And Robbie's imagination is more vivid than most kids', remember that too. And lots of kids have an imaginary playmate. Kids are different, he said, they have no control over their imaginations, they see things, hear things, stuff like that, and there's no reason anything like that should ever bother you. And besides, he'll grown out of it.

Margaret said she guessed he was right. They were standing side by side at the stove, both of them putting dinner on the table. Robbie was in the living room.

'And, you know,' David said, 'you're beginning to talk about this Alec as if you really did believe in him.'

Margaret, relieved at having gotten it all out, told it all out loud, laughed and said, 'No Alec, huh?'

'No Alec.'

She shrugged. 'Okay, then,' she said. 'No Alec.'

That was on Friday.

On Monday, David went back to working the night shift for a week.

On Monday evening, Margaret fed husband and son, then sent David off to work with a kiss. She stayed at the door until she saw the car disappear around the corner. Then she went inside to put Robbie to bed. She was relieved when he seemed to fall asleep at once.

When she returned to the kitchen, it was beginning to rain. She flicked on the yard lights for a second to see what had been left outside that might rust. Her eyes swept the yard. There was nothing. She took her time cleaning up after dinner. No rush tonight. Robbie was already asleep. Before she settled in front of the television with a bowl of Jell-O, she went around the house and made sure all the windows were closed. It was raining hard now.

The crash and scream from the bedroom sent her leaping off the couch. The glass bowl flew out of her hand. Her knee caught the edge of the coffee table. Pain shot through her leg.

Robbie!

She ran for the bedroom, stumbling against the wall, her injured knee barely supporting her.

'Robbie?'

The boy was standing in the crib, his hands gripping the top of the side, fingers curled tightly around the bar. He was looking past her, his gaze fixed.

'Robbie!'

She ran for him, swept him up out of the crib into her arms. She almost had to pull his hands free from the railing. As she gathered him in close to her pounding heart, his head swung away from her. He was still staring into the corner of the room beside the door.

Margaret patted him on the back, stroked him, soothed him.

'What happened, baby? What happened? Tell Mommy what happened?'

She turned from the crib to walk up and down the room with him, as she had done when he was an infant.

'Tell Mommy what happened.' She repeated the words over and over. 'Tell Mommy what happened.' She kept her face close to the boy's silken hair. 'Tell Mommy what happened.'

'Alec came inside,' Robbie said at last.

Margaret's knee hurt more now. She had forgotten it the instant Robbie was safely in her arms, but now the pain burned through her leg, shot down through the bone. She stumbled and had to tighten her grip on the boy as she turned toward the door. Robbie was squirming in her arms. She lost her balance and bumped her shoulder against the doorframe.

She carried Robbie out to the living room. He was stiff in her arms for a moment, as if reluctant to come, but he began to relax when she settled him on the couch beside her. She couldn't hold him in her lap the way she wanted because of the pain in her leg. She thought she could feel the knee already beginning to swell. She tried but she could coax nothing out of Robbie about what had happened, what the noise was, what had made him scream. His only response was a shrug. She felt him all over, his arms and legs, and looked in his eyes, felt his forehead. He was fine. But her examination of him made her realize even more strongly how much her own leg was hurting. It was more than half an hour now since she had struck it and the swelling was now painful itself.

It was almost another half hour before Robbie finally grew drowsy and Margaret felt it was safe to leave him alone on the couch. She made sure he wasn't going to wake up, then hobbled off to the kitchen for ice. She improvised an ice pack with a dish towel and started back to the living room.

But what had happened? She was sure she had heard a crash at the same instant Robbie had screamed. Or had she dreamed it? The rain was still lashing at the windows. She could hear the trees whipping in the wind. Maybe a branch had snapped outside. She'd been distracted by the television when it happened. Maybe her mind had joined all the sounds together.

Robbie was safely asleep on the couch. Margaret supported herself against the wall for a moment, then hobbled slowly down the hall to take one more look in the bedroom, just to be sure.

She flipped on the bright overhead light. Her gaze swept carefully around the room, cataloguing everything in its place, until she came to the corner at her left side.

The red fire truck was in the corner, the front end of it crushed against the wall. The wall itself was split with the impact. The ladders had flown off the truck and lay nearby. One of the wheels had come off. Another was bent askew on its axle and the remains of the truck leaned sideways. The front cab was mangled on one side, crushed almost flat on the other. A red stain soaked the rug beneath it.

'Oh my God!' Margaret said.

*Alec came inside.*

Then she heard the doorbell ring.

# Carl Shiffman
# The squatters

The girl sitting on one of the suitcases outside the front door stood up as she heard the sound of bolts being drawn back. She looked up at the front of the house as she waited. 'Seems almost too good to be true,' she said aloud.

The building – it was little more than a large cottage – had evidently been long empty of human habitation. The windows had a dusty set of drawn curtains at each of them. The sills were carpeted with dead leaves. A long stain on the grey stone wall showed where rainwater had flowed from a broken gutter.

The young man who pulled open the door was about the same age as she was: somewhere between eighteen and twenty. He could not have been called handsome – there was too much flabbiness in his face, and a weakness about his mouth – but he did have a striking appearance. It was not the black hair that fell almost to his shoulders that lent him this distinction, but the contrast between it and the clear paleness of his skin. His brown eyes stood out in that curious pallor as though set in a paper mask. But perhaps the most noticeable feature was the colour in his narrow lips: a lack of redness, at times almost a violet shade.

'What a find!' he said, gloatingly. He seized one of the cases and a haversack and began to carry them inside. 'This is our lucky day after all, Marje. Full of stuff, too – furniture, everything.'

Marjorie took up the rest of their luggage and limped into the narrow hall. She looked into the door on her right. 'How did you get in?'

Kevin pointed to the opposite door. 'In there. A side window.'

'You didn't break it, to get in, did you?'

'Course not! I know the law as well as you do. Didn't have to, anyway. It was wide open.'

The girl entered the room. Sure enough, there was a narrow

window looking out over a weed-tangled rose garden to the trees they had seen as they tramped along the coast road. 'Did you wade through a canal, or something?' She pointed to a row of footprints on the carpet; they ran from the window to the door.

'That wasn't me – they were there when I got in,' said Kevin, stooping to touch the nearest mark with a finger. 'Still wet, too. Someone's been in, and not so long ago either.' He took a heavy poker from the grate. 'Wait here a minute. I'll have a butcher's upstairs.' He went out, and she heard him climbing the stairs.

She sat down heavily in the fireside chair, but it was clammy and unpleasantly chill, and she moved instead to one of the wooden chairs at the table. Pulling off her shoe, she inspected the blister on her heel. It had been some two miles walk from Thornsea, and not one vehicle had stopped in response to Kevin's outstretched arm and jabbing thumb.

The expedition to Thornsea had been a fruitless one. One of the other squatters in the London house from which they had all been evicted had told them that the Suffolk village was 'full of empty cottages, just waiting to be moved into'. But there had only been three, two derelict shells and one directly opposite the local policeman's house. Discouraged and desolate, they had set off along the empty featureless coast road in search of a lift back to the city.

She heard Kevin's feet on the stairs, and stood up anxiously, but his expression was one of satisfaction and relief.

'No one about. Must have been an old tramp who broke in for a night's kip.'

'He must have been a bit simple, then,' Marjorie declared. 'I mean, nothing's been touched, and some of the stuff in here must be worth a few bob.'

Kevin shrugged. 'So, he was a rich tramp. Who cares? Main thing is, *we*'re in now, and no one can turn us out as long as we go by the book.'

They spent the rest of the day bringing bedding down from the bedroom to dry in front of the fire they lit in each of the rooms. There was no electricity, as the power had been cut off at the mains, but there was an ample supply of candles in the tiny kitchen at the back of the house.

There were only two bedrooms on the upper floor, the larger of

130

which, at the front, was too far gone in dampness to use. What had probably once been the third was now a bathroom.

'Must be quite old,' said Kevin knowledgeably when he had completed his inspection of their new home. Outside, he found a small outhouse which might have been a toilet, but which now contained a rusting cycle and some gardening tools.

Within a week the squatters had established themselves very comfortably indeed. By burning wood fires in every room they had dispelled the worst of the dampness. The Electricity Authority had been contacted, and had promised to reconnect the supply in the near future. Kevin used the bicycle to ferry groceries from the village shops. He also thumbed a lift into Saxmundham and there arranged with the Social Security offices that his benefit be transferred to his new address. There was an Employment Office nearby, but he did not go there, since he had long ago decided that working did not suit him.

Marjorie was still troubled by a vague feeling that the house was too fine a prize to be won so easily.

'You don't think they'll come back, do you?' she asked one night as they sat by the fire. Candles were dotted around the room, their flames dancing and flickering cheerfully.

'Who?' Kevin was trying to make out the telephone number of a local second-hand furniture dealer in the paper. 'The owners, you mean? No, not a chance, girl. Place has been empty for ages, by the look of it. Queer, isn't it, the way everything's been left, as though they cleared out all of a sudden?'

Marjorie collected her transistor and announced that she was going to bed. The discordant racket faded as she went upstairs, and ceased altogether after a time.

The boy jerked out of the half-doze he had fallen into as he sat staring into the fire. He rose, stretched, and went round the room blowing out the candles one by one.

In the hall he paused at the bottom of the stairs. The sound – it had made him think of something soft dragging on the floor – had seemed to come from the kitchen. He groped along the narrow passageway that led past the stairs, wishing he had left one candle alight to carry with him. His outspread fingers touched the doorway, and he moved slowly inside. If he could locate the big dresser on the left, he knew, there would be matches there.

Something cold and wet draped itself round his arm and brushed his face. He sprang back instantly, crying out with the shock of the unexpected contact, found the edge of the door, and threw himself out and down the hall.

A faint light appeared above him. Marjorie was standing on the little gallery that ran from the top of the stairs. The candle in her hand lighted her face with odd, upside-down shadows.

'What in God's name . . .? Kevin, you're shaking like a leaf. What's happened?'

He tried to speak, found that his teeth were rattling together, and clamped his jaws shut. At last he managed: 'Bring – bring the light down, will you?'

She reached the hall and took his arm. He held a hand to his chest.

'Have you hurt yourself, or what?'

'Something touched me. In there.'

She glanced nervously at the black cavern mouth of the kitchen. The light from her candle did not reach much past it. 'In the kitchen? What was it?'

Kevin took a deep breath. He shuddered. 'Dunno. It was wet and cold. I felt it in the dark.'

'Oh, you *silly* bastard! Fancy frightening me like that!' Astonishingly, she marched into the kitchen and returned holding up something that dripped. 'This,' she explained tersely, 'is one of your shirts. I washed it after tea and hung it up on the line in there to dry.'

He could only stare at the shirt in her hand, his shock turned in an instant to a feeling of utter foolishness. It would be useless, he knew, to attempt to convey the horror of that sudden clammy touch. 'You should have told me it was in there,' was all he could find to say, and he knew it was a feeble retort as soon as he made it.

His sourness had evaporated next morning, however, and he was able to smile ruefully at her hoots of laughter as she recalled his fright. Later in the morning he cycled off to Thornsea to make phone calls and buy more groceries.

Marjorie carefully locked the doors as he had instructed. 'No one can throw us out as long as we're in occupation,' he'd explained. 'That's the law.'

She wandered from room to room, luxuriating in the spacious

132

privacy that contrasted so much with the cramped overcrowding they had been used to in their last squat. As she entered the front room with the side window, however, she stopped, a look of disgust on her face. 'Phew, what a horrible stink.' The room was filled with an odour that reminded her of fish that had gone off. She opened both windows and lit a fire in the grate, suspecting that the damp had returned and was somehow causing the stench.

As she stood with her hands out to the flames, the silence rushed in on her, and she hurried to find her radio.

Kevin was pink-cheeked and breathless when he returned. The wind had been against him, he explained, emptying the bag of wares on to the kitchen table. 'I was talking to an old geezer in the pub,' he went on, 'what used to be a fisherman when the village still had fishing-boats. Some right tales he was telling me.'

'You didn't let on we were living in this place?'

'Oh, the whole village knows that by now. Nothing happens in a place this size without they get to know about it. It's like telepathy.'

'Wouldn't have thought much ever did happen in a place like this,' said Marjorie with the city-dweller's unawareness of country matters.

One of the stories told by the old fisherman came to Kevin's mind. 'You might be surprised. There was a girl here, once, about the end of the last century, who—' He remembered her unfeeling scorn of the night before, and caught himself. 'Well, all sorts of things happen.'

Marjorie was studying the printed slip he had brought back with the groceries. 'Here, is that what this little lot cost? No wonder people leave houses standing empty and get out, if that's what the local shops are charging.'

It was raining heavily next morning as she pulled on the thin coat that served as a dressing-gown and went down to make coffee. Her sudden cry brought Kevin padding to the landing. She looked up at him, wide-eyed.

'Kev – come down quick and look at this!' He scrambled into his jeans and t-shirt and ran down.

'I felt the draught when I passed the door,' she said. 'Take a look.' The side window was wide open, just as it had been that first day.

'So you left the window open last night,' he said irritably. 'Why drag me out of bed just to see that?'

'But I never left it open! And that's not what I'm on about

anyway.' Impatiently she grabbed his arm and pointed. 'Don't you see! The footprints – they've come back! Look!'

He stared at the prints that ran, as before, from the window to the door. There was a big dark pool of water just inside the window, where the rain had blown in, perhaps. He bent and touched the nearest mark, as he had done the first time. Marjorie struggled against a queer feeling that time had somehow run backwards.

Kevin straightened. 'I think I know what it is. You left the window open –' He raised a hand at her denial – 'all right, maybe I did, and forgot, maybe you did. Anyway, the rain got in, see, and made the carpet wet, and the prints reappeared. It's like –' he cast about for a convincing simile – 'well, like the way invisible ink comes back when you put the right chemical on.'

'I'm bloody sure I didn't leave the window open.' To his astonishment, he saw that she was near to tears. 'I don't like it, Kev. Let's leave – go back to London.'

'Leave? You're joking! Give up this place? We'd never find as good a squat in a month of Sundays, and you know it. You know what it's getting like in London now.'

Marjorie, defeated, was silent. At last she said grudgingly: 'All right, then. But do something about that window, will you?'

He found a hammer and drove two four-inch nails into the bottom rail of the sash and into the frame below.

'There,' he said triumphantly. 'Like to see anyone open that.' And as if to seal the operation, he placed a small table in front of the window. Outside, the rain had stopped; ragged clouds were hurrying over the bending trees on the other side of the wall. Made restless by the clearing skies, he dug over a large section of the back garden that day.

This unaccustomed exercise so tired him that he went early to bed and fell asleep almost at once.

He was dragged from sleep by an insistent tugging at his arm. Marjorie's voice was a hoarse whisper. 'Kevin, wake up! For God's sake wake up.'

'What is it now?' he groaned, rolling over and beginning to sit up. Moonlight slanted in through the window.

Marjorie hissed: 'Ssshh! Don't make a noise. Listen!'

He did so, but heard nothing. 'What—' he began, but Marjorie held up a finger.

'No,' she said, 'it's stopped now. It sounded like a window being forced.'

Kevin was half-way out of bed before she finished speaking.

She held out an arm to restrain him. 'No, Kevin, don't go! Don't leave me here on my own.'

He was stuffing his feet into his boots and tugging on a shirt, both at once. 'I've had about enough of this,' he said viciously. 'Someone's been trying to scare us, that's what it is – trying to get us out same as the last people here.'

He opened the door and stood listening for a moment, then slipped out and tiptoed down the stairs. Marjorie sat in bed with her knees drawn up to her chin and her arms clasped round them.

The scream, when it came, struck her like a blow, and she flinched. She found herself standing at the open door pulling on her coat. From somewhere below she heard a scuffling. She went to the landing and looked down with bright fearful eyes.

Kevin blundered from the doorway below and clutched at the stair-rail. Then he was on the stairs and floundering up them, staggering, clutching at the treads before him as he slipped. He gained the top and rushed unseeing past her. She looked once more down into the hall – there was nothing to be seen there, nothing but the pale moonlight – then hurried into the bedroom.

Kevin was crouching with his back to the side of the bed. His hands fluttered at his chest. From the corner of his mouth a long thread of spittle hung trembling. His face was not merely pale, as it normally was, but literally grey. His eyes were open to their widest extent, staring past her at something she could not see.

Nevertheless, she glanced over her shoulder as she entered, and put a chair with its back under the handle.

She knelt and took his hands. They fluttered like captive birds. 'Kevin! Kevin, it's me! What's wrong? What happened?'

She had not expected an answer, but his head rolled loosely until he was looking at her. Disturbingly, his head hung a little to one side, like that of an idiot.

'She was sitting in the chair at the fireside,' he said distinctly. 'I saw the white sleeve on the arm of it – you know it has a high back, and it's turned away from the door. So I only saw the white stuff on the chair arm.

'Made me mad, seeing that. Someone coming in, and calmly sitting there. I could see the window was open, you know, with the moon coming in through it. So I got hold of the back of the chair, and I gave it a shake.' He stopped and looked at Marjorie solemnly. 'You know, I think if I hadn't done that, it would have been all right. I think if you don't disturb her, she's all right. All . . . right. Just goes in and out, you know?'

'What are you talking about? Kevin! Kev – don't look like that. It frightens me. Oh, what's *wrong* with you?'

The idiot head regarded her without recognition. 'The old chap in the pub told me about her. She married a fisherman and he brought her here. Happy ever after, sort of thing. Only he drowned a few days after, see, and she was left all alone here. She went a bit funny, the old guy said. Started wandering along the shore in the evenings, in the dress she'd married in at the village church.

'She wasn't here when her family got here – she'd done herself in. Fancy that. Drowned herself, I suppose he meant; he said the weight of the wedding-dress would have kept the body under – well. She was never found, you see.'

He's given himself a fright like last time, thought Marjorie, only worse, much worse. It's like a stroke, almost. I wish he wouldn't look at me like that, as if I was someone else.

She said: 'I'll have to go and get a doctor. Kevin? Can you hear me? I'm going to try to get you into the bed. All right?'

She got him on to the bed and stood panting with the effort. He rolled his head on the pillow until the grey face was looking at her.

'When I shook the chair, she stood up and turned round, you know. In the moonlight. All dressed in white. And then – then she put up a hand and lifted the veil. I thought I would die when I saw her. If I see it – see her face again I *will* die.'

Marjorie had become convinced that if she could get a doctor to him, all would be well. But Thornsea was two miles away. How—? She remembered the old cycle in the shed. Dressing quickly, she took the chair from the door and stood looking for a moment at the figure on the bed.

Kevin said suddenly: 'The last people here had to go and disturb her. That's why they left so sudden, you see.'

Marjorie went out and down the stairs and kept her eyes fixed straight ahead on the front door. The top bolt was stiff and refused to move, and she tugged at it for an age, while her back tingled in the expectation of a bony hand on it. At last she had it open and she was out on the path and running to the shed where the cycle was kept.

Kevin drifted back to consciousness as the window changed from black to grey. Birds chirped and squawked on the newly-turned earth below. Kevin lay still, confused. He had had some awful nightmare, he knew, and even now he felt unsettled. Had he woken in the night?

Well, he had dreamed the bit about Marjorie going off for a doctor, at any rate, for she was here and sleeping beside him, with the sheet all pulled around her as usual.

No, not sleeping; she stirred and sat up. And not Marjorie either, but the white-clad dripping figure of his dream. Kevin threw himself back and a monstrous pain seared across his chest and arm. He saw – it was to be the last thing he ever saw – a thin gloved hand lift to raise the white veil. He had seen that fleshless face before, and it had driven him to the edge of his sanity.

He found that he was looking at the window upside-down, somehow, and that the sky was turning from grey to black.

Marjorie jumped from the doctor's car as he drew up at the front door. She waited impatiently as he collected his bag from the back seat and followed. As he entered the hall he wrinkled his nose in disgust. 'Something wrong with the drains,' he muttered to himself, 'or else the house is terribly damp.' The sun was just above the line where sea and sky met, and its light picked out the peeling wallpaper and the mildewed ceiling.

The girl was already at the door of the bedroom. The doctor, looking past her, saw the body that sprawled half-in and half-out of the double bed. 'Let me go in first,' he said, edging her aside.

He had to squeeze between the bed and the window to reach the boy's outflung arm and feel the wrist. Cardiac arrest, he thought, laying the arm back on the floor. He looked at the unwrinkled skin, the dark hair, the hands.

'How old was he?' he asked.

'Twenty.' Marjorie's face was blank, her voice dull. 'Is he dead?'

'I'm sorry, yes. Heart attack, I'd say at a guess, though it is very unusual in a man of that age. There will have to be an inquest.' He saw that one half of the bed was wet; touching it cautiously, he found the sheet was as cold as ice. 'How can people live in such conditions,' he reflected, 'in this day and age?'

Marjorie, unhearing, had walked unconsciously from the room and on to the little landing. The sun, higher and stronger now, threw its light in at the open front door and illuminated to her suddenly stricken gaze half-dried footprints on the wooden treads.

# Stephen King

# The woman in the room

The question is: Can he do it?

He doesn't know. He knows that she chews them sometimes, her face wrinkling at the awful orange taste, and a sound comes from her mouth like splintering popsicle sticks. But these are different pills . . . gelatin capsules. The box says DARVON COMPLEX on the outside. He found them in her medicine cabinet and turned them over in his hands, thinking. Something the doctor gave her before she had to go back to the hospital. Something for the ticking nights. The medicine cabinet is full of remedies, neatly lined up like a voodoo doctor's cures. Gris-gris of the Western world. FLEET SUP-POSITORIES. He has never used a suppository in his life and the thought of putting a waxy something in his rectum to soften by body heat makes him feel ill. There is no dignity in putting things up your ass. PHILLIPS MILK OF MAGNESIA. ANACIN ARTHRITIS PAIN FOR-MULA, PEPTO-BISMOL. More. He can trace the course of her illness through the medicines.

But these pills are different. They are like regular Darvon only in that they are grey gelatin capsules. But they are bigger, what his dead father used to call hosscock pills. The box says Asp. 350 gr, Darvon 100 gr, and could she chew them even if he was to give them to her? *Would* she? The house is still running; the refrigerator runs and shuts off, the furnace kicks in and out, every now and then the cuckoo bird pokes grumpily out of the clock to annnounce an hour or a half. He supposes that after she dies it will fall to Kevin and him to break up housekeeping. She's gone, all right. The whole house says so. She

is in the Central Maine Hospital, in Lewiston. Room 312. She went when the pain got so bad she could no longer go out to the kitchen and make her own coffee. At times, when he visited, she cried without knowing it.

The elevator creaks going up, and he finds himself examining the blue elevator certificate. The certificate makes it clear that the elevator is safe, creaks or no creaks. She has been here for nearly three weeks now and today they gave her an operation called a 'cortotomy'. He is not sure if that is how it's spelled, but that is how it sounds. The doctor has told her that the 'cortotomy' involves sticking a needle into her neck and then into her brain. The doctor has told her that this is like sticking a pin into an orange and spearing a seed. When the needle has poked into her pain centre, a radio signal will be sent down to the tip of the needle and the pain centre will be blown out. Like unplugging a TV. Then the cancer in her belly will stop being such a nuisance.

The thought of this operation makes him even more uneasy than the thought of suppositories melting warmly in his anus. It makes him think of a book by Michael Crichton called *The Terminal Man*, which deals with putting wires in people's heads. According to Crichton, this can be a very bad scene. You better believe it.

The elevator door opens on the third floor and he steps out. This is the old wing of the hospital, and it smells like the sweet-smelling sawdust they sprinkle over puke at a county fair. He has left the pills in the glove compartment of his car. He has not had anything to drink before this visit.

The walls up here are two-tone; brown on the bottom and white on top. He thinks that the only two-tone combination in the whole world that might be more depressing than brown and white would be pink and black. Hospital corridors like giant Good 'n' Plentys. The thought makes him smile and feel nauseated at the same time.

Two corridors meet in a T in front of the elevator, and there is a drinking fountain where he always stops to put things off a little. There are pieces of hospital equipment here and there, like strange playground toys. A litter with chrome sides and rubber wheels, the sort of thing they use to wheel you up to the 'OR' when they are ready to give you your 'cortotomy'. There is a large circular object whose function is unknown to him. It looks like the wheels you sometimes see in squirrel cages. There is a rolling IV tray with two bottles hung from it, like a Salvador Dali dream of tits. Down one of the two corridors is the nurses' station, and laughter fuelled by coffee drifts out to him.

He gets his drink and then saunters down towards her room. He is scared of what he may find and hopes she will be sleeping. If she is, he will not wake her up.

Above the door of every room there is a small square light. When a patient pushes his call button this light goes on, glowing red. Up and down the hall patients are walking slowly, wearing cheap hospital robes over their hospital underwear. The robes have blue and white pinstripes and round collars. The hospital underwear is called a 'johnny'. The 'johnnies' look all right on the women but decidedly strange on the men because they are like knee-length dresses or slips. The men always seem to wear brown imitation-leather slippers on their feet. The women favour knitted slippers with balls of yarn on them. His mother has a pair of these and calls them 'mules'.

The patients remind him of a horror movie called *The Night of the Living Dead*. They all walk slowly, as if someone had unscrewed the tops of their organs like mayonnaise jars and liquids were sloshing around inside. Some of them use canes. Their slow gait as they promenade up and down the halls is frightening but also dignified. It is the walk of people who are going nowhere slowly, the walk of college students in caps and gowns filing into a convocation hall.

Ectoplasmic music drifts everywhere from transitor radios. Voices babble. He can hear Black Oak Arkansas singing 'Jim Dandy' ('Go Jim Dandy, go Jim Dandy!' a falsetto voice screams merrily at the slow hall walkers). He can hear a talk-show host discussing Nixon in tones that have been dipped in acid like smoking quills. He can hear a polka with French lyrics – Lewiston is still a French-speaking town and they love their jigs and reels almost as much as they love to cut each other in the bars on lower Lisbon Street.

He pauses outside his mother's room and

for a while there he was freaked enough to come drunk. It made him ashamed to be drunk in front of his mother even though she was too doped and full of Elavil to know. Elavil is a tranquillizer they give to cancer patients so it won't bother them so much that they're dying.

The way he worked it was to buy two six-packs of Black Label beer at Sonny's Market in the afternoon. He would sit with the kids and watch their afternoon programmes on TV. Three beers with 'Sesame Street', two beers during 'Mister Rogers', one beer during 'Electric Company'. Then one with supper.

He took the other five beers in the car. It was a twenty-two-mile drive from Raymond to Lewiston, via Routes 302 and 202, and it was possible to be pretty well in the bag by the time he got to the hospital, with one or two beers left over. He would bring things for his mother and leave them in the car so there would be an excuse to go back and get them and also drink another half beer and keep the high going.

It also gave him an excuse to piss outdoors, and somehow that was the best of the whole miserable business. He always parked in the side lot, which was rutted, frozen November dirt, and the cold night air assured full bladder contraction. Pissing in one of the hospital bathrooms was too much like an apotheosis of the whole hospital experience: the nurse's call button beside the hopper, the chrome handle bolted at a 45-degree angle, the bottle of pink disinfectant over the sink. Bad news. You better believe it.

The urge to drink going home was nil. So leftover beers collected in the icebox at home and when there were six of them, he would

never have come if he had known it was going to be this bad. The first thought that crosses his mind is *She's no orange* and the second thought is *She's really dying quick now*, as if she had a train to catch out there in nullity. She is straining in the bed, not moving except for her eyes, but straining inside her body, something is moving in there. Her neck has been smeared orange with stuff that looks like Mercurochrome, and there is a bandage below her left ear where some humming doctor put the radio needle in and blew out sixty per cent of her motor controls along with the pain centre. Her eyes follow him like the eyes of a paint-by-the-numbers Jesus.

– I don't think you better see me tonight, Johnny. I'm not so good. Maybe I'll be better tomorrow.

– What is it?

– It itches. I itch all over. Are my legs together?

He can't see if her legs are together. They are just a raised V under the ribbed hospital sheet. It's very hot in the room. No one

142

is in the other bed right now. He thinks: Roommates come and roommates go, but my mom stays on for ever. Christ!

– They're together, Mom.

– Move them down, can you, Johnny? Then you better go. I've never been in a fix like this before. I can't move anything. My nose itches. Isn't that a pitiful way to be, with your nose itching and not able to scratch it?

He scratches her nose and then takes hold of her calves through the sheet and pulls them down. He can put one hand around both calves with no trouble at all, although his hands are not particularly large. She groans. Tears are running down her cheeks to her ears.

– Momma?

– Can you move my legs down?

– I just did.

– Oh. That's all right, then. I think I'm crying. I don't mean to cry in front of you. I wish I was out of this. I'd do anything to be out of this.

– Would you like a smoke?

– Could you get me a drink of water first, Johnny? I'm as dry as an old chip.

– Sure.

He takes her glass with a flexible straw in it out and around the corner to the drinking fountain. A fat man with an elastic bandage on one leg is sailing slowly down the corridor. He isn't wearing one of the pinstriped robes and is holding his 'johnny' closed behind him.

He fills the glass from the fountain and goes back to Room 312 with it. She has stopped crying. Her lips grip the straw in a way that reminds him of camels he has seen in travelogues. Her face is scrawny. His most vivid memory of her in the life he lived as her son is of a time when he was twelve. He and his brother Kevin and this woman had moved to Maine so that she could take care of her parents. Her mother was old and bedridden. High blood pressure had made his grandmother senile, and, to add insult to injury, had struck her blind. Happy eighty-sixth birthday. Here's one to grow on. And she lay in a bed all day long, blind and senile, wearing large diapers and rubber pants, unable to remember what breakfast had been but able to recite all the Presidents right up to Ike. And so the three generations of them had lived together in that house where he had so recently found the pills (although both grandparents are now long since dead) and at twelve he had been lipping off about something at the breakfast table, he doesn't remember what, but something, and his mother had been washing out her mother's pissy diapers and then running them through the wringer of her ancient washing machine, and she had turned around and laid into him with one of them, and the first snap of the wet, heavy diaper had upset his bowl of Special K and sent it spinning wildly across the table like a large blue tiddlywink, and the second blow had stropped his back, not hurting but stunning the smart talk out of his mouth and the woman now lying shrunken in this bed in this room had whopped him again and again, saying: You keep your big mouth *shut*, there's nothing big about you right now but your *mouth* and so you keep it shut until the rest of you grows the same *size*, and each italicized word was accompanied by a strop of his grandmother's wet diaper – *WHACKO!* – and any other smart things he might have had to say just evaporated. There was not a chance in the world for smart talk. He had discovered on that day and for all time that there is nothing in the world so perfect to set a twelve-year-old's impression of his place in the scheme of things into proper perspective as being beaten across the back with a wet grandmother-diaper. It had taken four years after that day to relearn the art of smarting off.

She chokes on the water a little and it frightens him even though he has been thinking about giving her pills. He asks her again if she would like a cigarette and she says:

– If it's not any trouble. Then you better go. Maybe I'll be better tomorrow.

He shakes a Kool out of one of the packages scattered on the table by her bed and lights it. He holds it between the first and second fingers of his right hand, and she puffs it, her lips stretching to grasp the filter. Her inhale is weak. The smoke drifts from her lips.

– I had to live sixty years so my son could hold my cigarettes for me.

– I don't mind.

She puffs again and holds the filter against her lips so long that he glances away from it to her eyes and sees they are closed.

– Mom?

The eyes open a little, vaguely.

– Johnny?

– Right.

– How long have you been here?

– Not long. I think I better go. Let you sleep.

– Hnnnnn.

He snuffs the cigarette in her ashtray and slinks from the room, thinking: I want to talk to that doctor. Goddamn it, I want to talk to the doctor who did that.

Getting into the elevator he thinks that the word 'doctor' becomes a synonym for 'man' after a certain degree of proficiency in the trade has been reached, as if it was an expected, provisioned thing that doctors must be cruel and thus attain a special degree of humanity. But

'I don't think she can really go on much longer,' he tells his brother later that night. His brother lives in Andover, seventy miles west. He only gets to the hospital once or twice a week.

'But is her pain better?' Kev asks.

'She says she itches.' He has the pills in his sweater pocket. His wife is safely asleep. He takes them out, stolen loot from his mother's empty house, where they all once lived with the grandparents. He turns the box over and over in his hand as he talks, like a rabbit's foot.

'Well then, she's better.' For Kev everything is always better, as if life moved towards some sublime vertex. It is a view the younger brother does not share.

'She's paralysed.'

'Does it matter at this point?'

'Of course it *matters!*' he bursts out, thinking of her legs under the white ribbed sheet.

'John, she's dying.'

'She's not dead yet.' This in fact is what horrifies him. The conversation will go around in circles from here, the profits accruing to the telephone company, but this is the nub. Not dead yet. Just lying in that room with a hospital tag on her wrist, listening to phantom radios up and down the hall. And

*

she's going to have to come to grips with time, the doctor says. He is a big man with a red, sandy beard. He stands maybe six foot four, and his shoulders are heroic. The doctor led him tactfully out into the hall when she began to nod off.

The doctor continues:

– You see, some motor impairment is almost unavoidable in an operation like the 'cortotomy'. Your mother has some movement in the left hand now. She may reasonably expect to recover her right hand in two to four weeks.

– Will she walk?

The doctor looks at the drilled-cork ceiling of the corridor judiciously. His beard crawls all the way down to the collar of his plaid shirt, and for some ridiculous reason Johnny thinks of Algernon Swinburne; why, he could not say. This man is the opposite of poor Swinburne in every way.

– I should say not. She's lost too much ground.

– She's going to be bedridden for the rest of her life?

– I think that's a fair assumption, yes.

He begins to feel some admiration for this man who he hoped would be safely hateful. Disgust follows the feeling; must he accord admiration for the simple truth?

– How long can she live like that?

– It's hard to say. (That's more like it.) The tumour is blocking one of her kidneys now. The other one is operating fine. When the tumour blocks it, she'll go to sleep.

– A uremic coma?

– Yes, the doctor says, but a little more cautiously. 'Uremia' is a techno-pathological term, usually the property of doctors and medical examiners alone. But Johnny knows it because his grandmother died of the same thing, although there was no cancer involved. Her kidneys simply packed it in and she died floating in internal piss up to her ribcage. She died in bed, at home, at dinnertime. Johhny was the one who first suspected she was truly dead this time, and not just sleeping in the comatose, open-mouthed way that old people have. Two small tears had squeezed out of her eyes. Her old toothless mouth was drawn in, reminding him of a tomato that has been hollowed out, perhaps to hold egg salad, and then left forgotten on the kitchen shelf for a stretch of days. He held

146

a round cosmetic mirror to her mouth for a minute, and when the glass did not fog and hide the image of her tomato mouth, he called for his mother. All of that had seemed as right as this did wrong.

– She says she still has pain. And that she itches.

The doctor taps his head solemnly, like Victor DeGroot in the old psychiatrist cartoons.

– She *imagines* the pain. But it is nonetheless real. Real to her. That is why time is so important. Your mother can no longer count time in terms of seconds and minutes and hours. She must restructure those units into days and weeks and months.

He realizes what this burly man with the beard is saying, and it boggles him. A bell dings softly. He cannot talk more to this man. He is a technical man. He talks smoothly of time, as though he has gripped the concept as easily as a fishing rod. Perhaps he has.

– Can you do anything more for her?

– Very little.

But his manner is serene, as if this were right. He is, after all, 'not offering false hope'.

– Can it be worse than a coma?

– Of course it *can*. We can't chart these things with any real degree of accuracy. It's like having a shark loose in your body. She may bloat.

– Bloat?

– Her abdomen may swell and then go down and then swell again. But why dwell on such things now? I believe we can safely say

that they would do the job, but suppose they don't? Or suppose they catch me? I don't want to go to court on a mercy-killing charge. Not even if I can beat it. I have no causes to grind. He thinks of newspaper headlines screaming MATRICIDE and grimaces.

Sitting is the parking lot, he turns the box over and over in his hands. DARVON COMPLEX. The question still is: *Can he do it?* Should he? She has said: *I wish I were out of this. I'd do anything to be out of this.* Kevin is talking of fixing her a room at his house so she won't die in the hospital. The hospital wants her out. They gave her some new pills and she went on a raving bummer. That was four days after the 'cortotomy'. They'd like her someplace else because no one has perfected a really foolproof 'cancerectomy' yet. And at this point if they got it all out of her she'd be left with nothing but her legs and her head.

He has been thinking of how time must be for her, like something that has gotten out of control, like a sewing basket full of threaded spools spilled all over the floor for a big mean tomcat to play with. The days in Room 312. The nights in Room 312. They have run a string from the call button and tied it to her left index finger because she can no longer move her hand far enough to press the button if she thinks she needs the bedpan.

It doesn't matter too much anyway because she can't feel the pressure down there; her midsection might as well be a sawdust pile. She moves her bowels in the bed and pees in the bed and only knows when she smells it. She is down to ninety-five pounds from one-fifty and her body's muscles are so unstrung that it's only a loose bag tied to her brain like a child's sack puppet. Would it be any different at Kev's? Can he do murder? He knows it is murder. The worst kind, matricide, as if he were a sentient foetus in an early Ray Bradbury horror story, determined to turn the tables and abort the animal that has given it life. Perhaps it is his fault anyway. He is the only child to have been nurtured inside her, a change-of-life baby. His brother was adopted when another smiling doctor told her she would never have any children of her own. And of course, the cancer now in her began in the womb like a second child, his own darker twin. His life and her death began in the same place. Should he not do what the other is doing already, so slowly and clumsily?

He has been giving her aspirin on the sly for the pain she *imagines* she has. She has them in a Sucrets box in her hospital-table drawer, along with her get-well cards and her reading glasses that no longer work. They have taken away her dentures because they are afraid she might pull them down her throat and choke on them, so now she simply sucks the aspirin until her tongue is slightly white.

Surely he could give her the pills; three or four would be enough. Fourteen hundred grains of aspirin and four hundred grains of Darvon administered to a woman whose body weight has dropped thirty-three per cent over five months.

No one knows he has the pills, not Kevin, not his wife. He thinks that maybe they've put someone else in Room 312's other bed and he won't have to worry about it. He can cop out safely. He wonders if that wouldn't be best, really. If there is another woman in the room, his options will be gone and he can regard the fact as a nod from Providence. He thinks

— You're looking better tonight.
— Am I?
— Sure. How do you feel?
— Oh, not so good. Not so good tonight.
— Let's see you move your right hand.

She raises it off the counterpane. It floats splay-fingered in front of her eyes for a moment, then drops. Thump. He smiles and she smiles back. He asks her,

— Did you see the doctor today?
— Yes, he came in. He's good to come every day. Will you give me a little water, John?

He gives her some water from the flexible straw.

— You're good to come as often as you do, John. You're a good son.

She's crying again. The other bed is empty, accusingly so. Every now and then one of the blue and white pinstriped bathrobes sails by them up the hall. The door stands open half-way. He takes the water gently away from her, thinking idiotically: Is this glass half empty or half full?

— How's your left hand?
— Oh, pretty good.
— Let's see.

She raises it. It has always been her smart hand, and perhaps that is why it has recovered as well as it has from the devastating effects of the 'cortotomy'. She clenches it. Flexes it. Snaps the fingers weakly. Then it falls back to the counterpane. Thump. She complains,

— But there's no feeling in it.
— Let me see something.

He goes to her wardrobe, opens it, and reaches behind the coat she came to the hospital in to get at her purse. She keeps it in here because she is paranoid about robbers; she has heard that some of the orderlies are rip-off artists who will lift anything they can get their hands on. She has heard from one of her roommates who has since gone home that a woman in the new wing lost five hundred dollars which she kept in her shoe. His mother is paranoid about a great many things lately, and has once told him a man sometimes hides under her bed in the late-at-night. Part of it is the combination of drugs they are trying on her. They make the bennies he occasionally dropped in college look like Excedrin. You can have your pick from the locked drug cabinet at the end of the corridor just past the nurses' station: ups and downs, highs and bummers. Death, maybe, merciful death like a sweet black blanket. The wonders of modern science.

He takes the purse back to her bed and opens it.

– Can you take something out of here?

– Oh, Johnny, I don't know . . .

He says persuasively:

– Try it. For me.

The left hand rises from the counterpane like a crippled helicopter. It cruises. Dives. Comes out of the purse with a single wrinkled Kleenex. He applauds:

– Good! Good!

But she turns her face away.

– Last year I was able to pull two full dish trucks with these hands.

If there's to be a time, it's now. It is very hot in the room but the sweat on his forehead is cold. He thinks: If she doesn't ask for aspirin, I won't. Not tonight. And he knows if it isn't tonight it's never. Okay.

Her eyes flick to the half-open door slyly.

– Can you sneak me a couple of my pills, Johnny?

It is how she always asks. She is not supposed to have any pills outside of her regular medication because she has lost so much body weight and she has built up what his druggie friends of his college days would have called 'a heavy thing'. The body's immunity stretches to within a fingernail's breadth of lethal dosage. One more pill and you're over the edge. They say it is what happened to Marilyn Monroe.

– I brought some pills from home.

– Did you?

– They're good for pain.

He holds the box out to her. She can only read very close. She frowns over the large print and then says,

150

– I had some of that Darvon stuff before. It didn't help me.

– This is stronger.

Her eyes rise from the box to his own. Idly she says,

– Is it?

He can only smile foolishly. He cannot speak. It is like the first time he got laid, it happened in the back of some friend's car and when he came home his mother asked him if he had a good time and he could only smile this same foolish smile.

– Can I chew them?

– I don't know. You could try one.

– All right. Don't let them see.

He opens the box and pries the plastic lid off the bottle. He pulls the cotton out of the neck. Could she do all that with the crippled helicopter of her left hand? Would they believe it? He doesn't know. Maybe they don't either. Maybe they wouldn't even care.

He shakes six of the pills into his hand. He watches her watching him. It is many too many, even she must know that. If she says anything about it, he will put them all back and offer her a single Arthritis Pain Formula.

A nurse glides by outside and his hand twitches, clicking the grey capsules together, but the nurse doesn't look in to see how the 'cortotomy kid' is doing.

His mother doesn't say anything, only looks at the pills like they were perfectly ordinary pills (if there is such a thing). But on the other hand, she has never liked ceremony; she would not crack a bottle of champagne on her own boat.

– Here you go,

he says in a perfectly natural voice, and pops the first one into her mouth.

She gums it reflectively until the gelatin dissolves, and then she winces.

– Taste bad? I won't . . .

– No, not too bad.

He gives her another. And another. She chews them with that same reflective look. He gives her a fourth. She smiles at him and he sees with horror that her tongue is yellow. Maybe if he hits her in the belly she will bring them up. But he can't. He could never hit his mother.

– Will you see if my legs are together?

– Just take these first.

He gives her a fifth. And a sixth. Then he sees if her legs are together. They are. She says,

– I think I'll sleep a little now.

– All right. I'm going to get a drink.

– You've always been a good son, Johnny.

He puts the bottle in the box and tucks the box into her purse, leaving the plastic top on the sheet beside her. He leaves the open purse beside her and thinks: *She asked for her purse. I brought it to her and opened it just before I left. She said she could get what she wanted out of it. She said she'd get the nurse to put it back in the wardrobe.*

He goes out and gets his drink. There is a mirror over the fountain, and he runs out his tongue and looks at it.

When he goes back into the room, she is sleeping with her hands pressed together. The veins in them are big, rambling. He gives her a kiss and her eyes roll behind their lids, but do not open.

Yes.

He feels no different, either good or bad.

He starts out of the room and thinks of something else. He goes back to her side, takes the bottle out of the box, and rubs it all over his shirt. The he presses the limp fingertips of her sleeping left hand on the bottle. Then he puts it back and goes out of the room quickly, without looking back.

He goes home and waits for the phone to ring and wishes he had given her another kiss. While he waits, he watches TV and drinks a lot of water.

152

# Barbara-Jane Crossley
# Black silk

Melvin, at thirty-seven, was rather proud of his success in life. Through sheer unrelenting hard work he had achieved a reputation in the fashion business for a constantly changing range of designs that were not only top quality but achievably-priced and sought after.

Sophistication was his hallmark, coupled with practicality and flair. Women who wore his clothes – and there were an ever-increasing number of them – were confident and independent, often in business, yet possessing a soft, sensuous underside which he also clothed admirably in his new line of seductive bedroom-wear.

He now had a chain of twenty-two shops, mostly in and around the capital, but his forays around the country made him hungry to expand further. All those potential markets going untapped in the provinces were more tempting than he could bear.

It was on one of his trips to set up a new shop in Scotland that he first met Tania. Always on the lookout for designing talent, he had asked his associates if they knew of any new names north of the border who were worth developing.

The beautiful Tania Stephanos was the result. Melvin – until now too engrossed in his burgeoning business affairs to give much time to women as anything more than clothes-horses – was captivated.

She first approached him across the floor of his half-finished new shop. Wood slats, textiles, paint and paper were everywhere. Decorators and joiners filled the room with their voices, hammerings and paint-slapping.

But when Tania walked across the floor it seemed to Melvin that everything else stopped. She was riveting. Tall and slender, her sleek dark hair swept up gracefully to reveal a perfect, astonishing face. For although her features were classically beautiful, they defied convention.

Her aspect was dominated by the eyes, to which the rest of her face seemed subservient. They were large, dark-lashed and mesmerizing, the irises glinting amber and gold round the bottomless pools of the pupils.

He was entranced. She introduced herself with a cool handshake. 'Hello. I know you are Mr de Ryan. My name is Tania Stephanos. I was told you were interested in new designers.'

Melvin could hardly contain himself. If her designs had come out like potato-sacks he would have declared them the most stunning innovation since the New Wave and launched them with a million pounds. But he could see that if her own clothes were anything to go by they would not only be distinctive and striking but tasteful, tempting, and above all marketable.

She wore a blouse of shiny black silk embroidered with a delicate tracery of patterns that could only be of her own making. Her skirt was cut like an aerodynamic dream, catching each breath of air to swathe itself lightly round her svelte hips and her legs were sheened in silk stockings of the finest thread.

Her eyes smiled back at him, knowing she had made an impression. He pulled himself together, took her arm as though their intimacy were already established and guided her through the piles of material to the door.

Their affairs would be better discussed over a good lunch, he told her, and bore her off in his Jaguar to a restaurant with high accolades for its culinary delights and a cool indifference to thoughts of economy.

She in turn was impressed. And as the meal progressed they learned a great deal about each other. Tania was thirty, a widow, having only just settled in Britain after her Scottish-born husband had died, she told him with contained emotion, of a massive heart-attack in her native Venezuela.

She and her husband had been beginning their own fashion business but after he died, she could do nothing for months, drowned in a black emptiness of loss. She was only just beginning to gather up the threads of her life again. She smiled as she spoke, her eyes deep and warm and beckoning, and Melvin fell into them like a willing slave.

His side of the story was one of quest, always for the best – in beauty and in business he knew he had to come out on top. And now, with this remarkable woman in front of him it seemed as though he had reached the pinnacle. He had to have her, he knew he had. But he was determined to do it properly – not in the quick, callow fashion of some of his colleages who would flit straight from boardroom to bedroom with scarecely a qualm.

His courtship was lavish and extravagant. He sent her so many roses she had to leave some in the bath, and perfume enough to bathe in. Before long he had asked her not only to marry him but to become his business partner and in due course she assented with smiling pleasure.

Meanwhile, her designs were coming off the drawing board at an astonishing pace. He was ever more intrigued at their originality and inspiration, combining South American mystique with Scottish boldness. He was convinced their new lines would be the best sellers yet.

He noticed her penchant for silk in many of her creations. She seemed to revel in its smooth feel against the skin and delight in its subtle sheen. As an indulgence he bought her a very expensive and richly-coloured dress of finest quality Chinese silk and presented it to her in glowing expectation of her grateful pleasure. But, to his surprise, she turned it down.

Tactfully, but firmly, she told him she only wore her own silk next to her skin, silk she had woven herself with her own hands. He was further impressed – he never realized her practical skills extended to this.

It only served to make him want her the more. With difficulty he resisted all temptation to take her to bed before their wedding night and began to look forward to it with heavy-breathed anticipation.

As they planned to be married in Scotland they decided to spend the first night of their honeymoon in her large and roomy apartment. He did not want their first night together to be spoiled by the exhaustion of long travel. The following day they would depart for St Lucia.

The wedding was one of the society events of the seaon – reported in gossip columns and with invitations jealously sought. After the celebrations were over they arrived, exhausted but alone together at last, in her lavishly-appointed apartment.

The day's champagne had only served to sharpen Melvin's sexual senses as they each began to undress. He was rather surprised to see that under her white dress – silk of course – she was wearing not white but black underwear. She saw his look – 'I always wear it,' she laughed. 'It makes me feel better.'

Indeed it was the most beautiful shape, setting off her breasts and body in a scant, tantalizing concoction of midnight lace.

He took her in his arms and held her close. So near, nearer than he had ever been before. She was warm, melting, enveloping in her embrace.

She gently pushed him away to turn and draw back the sheets. He registered more surprise. For they too were of black silk. He smiled indulgently at her obsession and drew her down with him on to the pillows.

Feeling her body smooth and soft against him was almost more than he could endure. The heat rose up in him and he could hardly contain it. Quickly he felt the underwear tearing away from her as he desperately sought to complete the act.

As his imprisoned love found its release it soared upwards, hot and passionate, to the peak, the highest pinnacle, the end of his quest. And slowly, softly, his body dropped, spent on to the pillow.

She was all he had ever dreamed of, he had achieved perfection.

As he looked over to take his fill of her again he was astonished to see her keening over him with her enormous eyes. He had never seen anyone or anything looking like that before.

And suddenly looking down at her he noticed something moving on her skin. Something black and spiky. It looked – no it could not be – it looked like a small but finely-haired spider crawling up her smooth abdomen.

Casting her eyes down she watched it crawl with a steady smile. Taking it on her hand she caressed it. And suddenly he noticed another on her thigh, and more and more seeming to come up from the end of the bed.

'How do you like my babies?' she purred. 'Aren't they beautiful? They spin for me, you know, beautiful silken webs for my beautiful silken garments, don't you my pretties, my darling ones.'

Horrified, he whirled from the bed, but found himself tangled in the clinging sheets.

156

'No you don't,' came the low, growling voice. 'I have you now, Mr Melvin de Ryan. The doors are locked and I have hidden the key. You are trapped in my mesh for ever.'

He turned to stare at her in terror. The creeping, palpating black insects were smothering her legs like a glittering gown.

Then he screamed as he realized his end. Everyone knew the punishment female spiders executed on their mates after copulation. Her perfect teeth were gleaming amid the encroaching blanket of black.

Paralysed, he was helpless. Her mouth was gaping wide, growing into mandibles, ready to tear upon him in greedy succulence. She fastened on his stomach, bore down upon his groin and the more he struggled the more the web of sheeting fastened him down.

The pain grew beyond his endurance, sending hot searing spears through his ravaged body. Before he passed out into oblivion he remembered with grim appal the gossip columnists' favourite name for his lovely wife: The Black Widow was at her work once more.

selected by Herbert van Thal
## The 22nd Pan Book of Horror Stories £1.50

Fourteen tales of stark and loathsome nightmare to people the dark hours with the most hideous of imaginings . . . 'he gazed at the tongue embedded in a sea of froth' – 'Sideshow'; 'a richly seasoned liver pâté obtained from the corpse of an unknown racing driver' – 'Dante's Bistro'; 'two of the man's fingers fell into the gutter.' – 'The Singer Not the Throng'; 'the fetid odour of ageing flesh rose from the bedclothes. 'Good morning, Mummy,' said the hag' – 'The Clock'.

Frank de Felitta
## The Entity £2.50

Carlotta Moran, a widow with three children, still young and attractive enough to build a new life – until something hideous enters her world. To the psychiatrists she is deranged, a hysteric on the brink of schitzophrenia – to the psychic researchers her experiences are beyond the credibility of science . . . Night after night a formless malevolence posseses her – a sexual scavenger from the outer reaches of the unknown . . . .

The ultimate novel of supernatural terror and sexual horror.

Thomas Tessier
## Phantom £1.75

Ned was only a kid, but he knew. There were forces that stalked the night. Like that night in Washington when his mother almost died and he heard them. In the house, at dead of night he heard them. Then they moved to the tiny seacoast town of Lynnington, and he still knew, even there, something was coming after him. In the end Ned must face the terror alone. He must seek out the phantoms on their own ground and fight them for his very soul. Through a long night of cataclysmic battle . . .

## Fiction

| | | |
|---|---|---|
| The Chains of Fate | Pamela Belle | £2.95p |
| Options | Freda Bright | £1.50p |
| The Thirty-nine Steps | John Buchan | £1.50p |
| Secret of Blackoaks | Ashley Carter | £1.50p |
| Hercule Poirot's Christmas | Agatha Christie | £1.50p |
| Dupe | Liza Cody | £1.25p |
| Lovers and Gamblers | Jackie Collins | £2.50p |
| Sphinx | Robin Cook | £1.25p |
| My Cousin Rachel | Daphne du Maurier | £1.95p |
| Flashman and the Redskins | George Macdonald Fraser | £1.95p |
| The Moneychangers | Arthur Hailey | £2.50p |
| Secrets | Unity Hall | £1.75p |
| Black Sheep | Georgette Heyer | £1.75p |
| The Eagle Has Landed | Jack Higgins | £1.95p |
| Sins of the Fathers | Susan Howatch | £3.50p |
| Smiley's People | John le Carré | £1.95p |
| To Kill a Mockingbird | Harper Lee | £1.95p |
| Ghosts | Ed McBain | £1.75p |
| The Silent People | Walter Macken | £1.95p |
| Gone with the Wind | Margaret Mitchell | £3.50p |
| Blood Oath | David Morrell | £1.75p |
| The Night of Morningstar | Peter O'Donnell | £1.75p |
| Wilt | Tom Sharpe | £1.75p |
| Rage of Angels | Sidney Sheldon | £1.95p |
| The Unborn | David Shobin | £1.50p |
| A Town Like Alice | Nevile Shute | £1.75p |
| Gorky Park | Martin Cruz Smith | £1.95p |
| A Falcon Flies | Wilbur Smith | £2.50p |
| The Grapes of Wrath | John Steinbeck | £2.50p |
| The Deep Well at Noon | Jessica Stirling | £2.50p |
| The Ironmaster | Jean Stubbs | £1.75p |
| The Music Makers | E. V. Thompson | £1.95p |

## Non-fiction

| | | |
|---|---|---|
| The First Christian | Karen Armstrong | £2.50p |
| Pregnancy | Gordon Bourne | £3.50p |
| The Law is an Ass | Gyles Brandreth | £1.75p |
| The 35mm Photographer's Handbook | Julian Calder and John Garrett | £5.95p |
| London at its Best | Hunter Davies | £2.95p |
| Back from the Brink | Michael Edwardes | £2.95p |

| | | |
|---|---|---|
| ☐ **Travellers' Britain** | } Arthur Eperon | £2.95p |
| ☐ **Travellers' Italy** | | £2.95p |
| ☐ **The Complete Calorie Counter** | Eileen Fowler | 80p |
| ☐ **The Diary of Anne Frank** | Anne Frank | £1.75p |
| ☐ **And the Walls Came Tumbling Down** | Jack Fishman | £1.95p |
| ☐ **Linda Goodman's Sun Signs** | Linda Goodman | £2.50p |
| ☐ **Scott and Amundsen** | Roland Huntford | £3.95p |
| ☐ **Victoria RI** | Elizabeth Longford | £4.95p |
| ☐ **Symptoms** | Sigmund Stephen Miller | £2.50p |
| ☐ **Book of Worries** | Robert Morley | £1.50p |
| ☐ **Airport International** | Brian Moynahan | £1.75p |
| ☐ **Pan Book of Card Games** | Hubert Phillips | £1.95p |
| ☐ **Keep Taking the Tabloids** | Fritz Spiegl | £1.75p |
| ☐ **An Unfinished History of the World** | Hugh Thomas | £3.95p |
| ☐ **The Baby and Child Book** | Penny and Andrew Stanway | £4.95p |
| ☐ **The Third Wave** | Alvin Toffler | £2.95p |
| ☐ **Pauper's Paris** | Miles Turner | £2.50p |
| ☐ **The Psychic Detectives** | Colin Wilson | £2.50p |
| ☐ **The Flier's Handbook** | | £5.95p |

All these books are available at your local bookshop or newsagent, or can be ordered direct from the publisher. Indicate the number of copies required and fill in the form below

1

..........................................................................................................................

Name_____

(Block letters please)

Address_____

_____

Send to CS Department, Pan Books Ltd, PO Box 40, Basingstoke, Hants
Please enclose remittance to the value of the cover price plus:
35p for the first book plus 15p per copy for each additional book ordered
to a maximum charge of £1.25 to cover postage and packing
Applicable only in the UK

While every effort is made to keep prices low, it is sometimes necessary to increase prices at short notice. Pan Books reserve the right to show on covers and charge new retail prices which may differ from those advertised in the text or elsewhere